KATHLEEN

Candice F. Ransom

SCHOLASTIC INC.
New York Toronto London Auckland Sydney Tokyo

KATHLEEN

A *SUNFIRE* Book

For Ann Reit
who took a chance on me

Chapter One

A freezing fog rolled in from the bay, softening the sea-scoured rocks and shrouding the people huddled on the dock. The fog muffled the mewling cries of gulls gliding overhead on idle wing.

Kathleen O'Connor clutched the frayed edges of the blanket tighter around her shoulders and scuffed her feet over the rough boards of the wharf in a feeble attempt to get warm.

My feet will be frozen forever, she thought, trying to remember the last time she had sat before the fire at home. Ten or eleven days ago? Kathleen tried to figure out the date — today should be February 7, 1847, but she wasn't sure.

"What's taking so long? Why won't they let us on the boat?" Mary O'Connor plucked absently at her daughter's sleeve.

Mary O'Connor's thick chestnut curls, wind-loosened from the scarf, snaked around her pale face, but the woman made no move to push her hair back. Her green eyes, the hue of the water churning in Sligo Bay, gazed sightlessly at the bustling activity on the dock.

She should be out of this cold, Kathleen observed. *Tucked in a nice warm bed with some hot oatmeal.* But she knew that it would take more than a bed and a bowl of oatmeal to help her mother, who still grieved for her three youngest children.

Devlin . . . Kerry . . . and the baby, Meara. She could scarcely believe that they were gone. . . . A sharp blast of wind lashed strands of Kathleen's ginger hair across her face in stinging whips, blowing away thoughts of her little brother and sisters.

A tall, gaunt figure in flapping rags approached them through the fog. Kathleen started for an instant. Appearing out of the mysterious mist that way, her father reminded her of the ghost of an ancient High King.

But as he drew closer, Liam O'Connor resembled a scarecrow more than a phantom Irish king. His sunken cheeks and deeply socketed gray eyes were grim badges to the past weeks of too little food, too many worries.

"That's our boat there," Liam told his wife and daughter when he joined them. He

MURFY FOR AMERIKY painted across one end, knock an old woman out of his way. Children wailed as they were separated from their mothers.

"All those people!" Kathleen gasped as she pulled her mother along. "How will we all fit on the boat?"

Just then, a man in hobnailed boots trod on Kathleen's foot. She glared at him, but he was soon lost in the crowd. Mary moved woodenly, as though sleepwalking, allowing Kathleen to lead her like a docile lamb. An overturned barrow of rotted cabbages caused Kathleen to trip and fall.

"Hurry, Katie!" her father called from the deck. "They're taking up the plank!"

They can't pull the gangway up so soon, Kathleen thought with horror. Hordes of passengers still clamored to board. As the people around her screamed and trampled others in their panic, Kathleen shoved her mother ahead. She was at the end of the pier now. Men scrambled up the sides of the ship, as dockworkers pulled the gangplank away from the dock, even though people hung on.

Kathleen's heart was in her throat. They had to get on that ship! It was their last chance for survival. By now, their landlord would have issued the order to have their old cottage torn down, so there was nothing to go back to.

Liam stood on the deck above them, leaning over the rail. "Hold it!" he shouted to the sailor nearest him. "Our passage was paid

5

leave, either. But even if their landlord hadn't evicted them, there was no reason to stay in Ireland. Not since Rory had died.

Behind them, passengers talked and joked, and many were dancing. They were so overjoyed to be leaving a country that offered no hope.

"Line up!" a man shouted, his heavy boots clumping over the deck. "Have yer tickets ready!"

While Kathleen waited in line next to her parents, she was unable to hold back memories of the nightmare — and Rory — any longer. During the long journey to Sligo, she'd kept her thoughts locked in a box, knowing if she lifted the lid and let herself remember, she would collapse in the road and cry for a life lost forever.

It had begun two years before, in 1845. That summer was unusually warm and humid. Kathleen spent the long twilight hours climbing the hills around Lake Maske, holding hands with Rory. They gazed over the cool, lapping waters and talked of their future together.

Rory Limerick. Straight black hair and eyes bluer than the lake. And his voice . . . no finer tenor could be found in County Mayo, or the whole of Ireland, for that matter. Whenever he sang, Kathleen thought of the rich, rolling moor, of a single seabird soaring against an endless sky.

Once that summer Rory took Kathleen to Carrowaglogh, where the timeworn land still

She remembered standing in the field with her father, surrounded by rotting plants and a horrible stench. "It's really bad, isn't it, Da?"

"Aye." Liam O'Connor dropped a shriveled black lump on the ground. "We are in great trouble, no doubt about that. This is what happens when a man tries to raise his family on what will grow on an acre-and-a-half farm, if you can call it that. I recollect my grandpa telling of the fine big farms the O'Connors once tilled. Weren't those the days? But that was before the English came over and took away our land."

Kathleen nodded. She knew that many years ago, rich Englishmen were given large parcels of property by the British government and that the Irish farms got smaller and smaller. Moreover, the Irish farmers no longer owned the land but were reduced to tenants, paying rent to an English landlord.

Liam O'Connor grew wheat, which he sold to pay the rest to Lord Reginald Wyndham, their landlord who lived in a fine house called Grimsby Hall, somewhere in the distant reaches of England. Potatoes were planted on the remaining land. They were cheap, grew easily in the damp bogs, and fed the entire O'Connor family for a full year, if the crop was good.

Looking over the ruined field, Kathleen felt a cold stab of fear. What would happen to them without potatoes?

Liam patted his daughter's shoulder.

Christmas, Kerry came down with the dreaded famine fever. With no food, no medicine, and no physician, eleven-year-old Kerry had little chance for recovery. She died on New Year's Eve, followed by Devlin, who had caught the fever from his sister.

Before the new year of 1847 was a week old, Kathleen received word that Rory was also ill. She ran outside immediately and down the lane bordered by walls of unmortared stone that divided the Limerick farm from the O'Connors'.

The Limerick cabin, made of mud, had been built in the cutaway side of a hill. Snow lay wetly on the thatched roof. The meager stack of peat outside the door filled Kathleen with alarm. Hadn't Rory been able to cut turf? The wet brown clumps had to be dug from bogs, then stacked to dry before burning. Without peat, their only fuel, the Irish would freeze.

Eight people lived in the cramped hut, but when Kathleen entered, she was acutely aware of emptiness. There was no furniture, not even a stool by the smoky fire that had been laid in the center of the clay floor.

A hollow-eyed wraith came forward. . . . No, it was Rory's grandmother.

Kathleen swallowed. "Where is he?" she asked, trying not to get too close to the old woman.

Granny Limerick pointed one twiglike arm to the corner. There was Rory.

He lay in crumpled bedding, moaning and

from Russia made travel by boat or horse and cart impossible — not that Kathleen's family had money for either. The three of them walked more than sixty miles from their village, north to Sligo.

"Only a little farther," Liam coaxed his wife and daughter when they cried to stop. "Just to that log there. That's not so far, is it? When we get on that boat to America, we'll be able to rest. And such grand meals we'll have. Potato stew three times a day!"

Kathleen shut out the bone-numbing cold and hunger and sights of the other wanderers who flocked like lost sheep by concentrating on the road ahead. She forced herself to forget those long evenings strolling along the shores of the lake, listening to Rory talk about the fine cottage they'd build when they were married, the wonderful life they'd have together. She tried to shut her eyes to the suffering she saw at every step of the long journey to Sligo. But she did not awaken from the nightmare. Ireland was dying.

By placing one foot before the other, hour after hour, mile after mile, day after day, Kathleen made it to Sligo, where boats bound for faraway places were moored. In Sligo Bay, her destiny lay —

"I asked yer name, miss," a harsh voice grated into her thoughts, yanking her sharply back to the present. "D'ye understand English? Or d'ye speak that pagan jibberish like the others?"

"Her and every other passenger on this ship," the man said, moving on to the next person in line.

Tickets were checked to make certain there were no stowaways on board, then the undesirable passengers — those without the fare or too ill to travel, Kathleen supposed — were ordered to line up away from the others.

A tug came alongside the *Griffin*, and the hapless undesirables, screaming and crying, were forced to jump over the rail onto the deck of the waiting tug, which would take them back to Sligo.

Next to Kathleen, Mary suddenly sagged, as though she was going to faint. Liam put his arm around his wife's waist.

"She's ready to drop," he said to Kathleen.

"Da, if she looks sick, they might put her ashore with the others!"

Liam looked pained. "Surely they must have a doctor on board. See what you can do."

Kathleen took one look at her mother's gray pallor, her chestnut hair incongruously bright, and ran after the officer who had questioned them. She had to clutch his arm before he acknowledged her presence.

"What d'ye want? Ye're supposed to be down below with the others."

"It's my mother, sir. She's ill. Can the doctor come?"

The man laughed harshly, blowing rum-laced breath in her face. "So ye want a doctor, do ye? An' I suppose you'd like to have 'er meals served on a silver platter?" He

sight of Ireland. She wanted to see her homeland as long as she could.

"Can I stand by the rail?" she asked. "I won't be in the way, I promise —"

"If I let you, the others'll want to. Passengers stay belowdecks. Now move."

Kathleen walked reluctantly toward the ladder leading into the hold. She cast one last look behind her, at land as richly green and tempting as a cask of emeralds.

She would never see their cottage in the bog again, never sit by a fragrant turf fire eating a bowl of potatoes and listening to Liam tell tales to the children. And she would never touch Rory's hand or brush back the coltish lock of hair from his forehead. Or see his love for her shining in his blue eyes.

Suddenly, it did not matter to her whether that ship sailed to America or roamed the Atlantic till eternity. Without Rory, her life was over.

self, and two elderly sisters from County Cork. Liam slept on the inside, next to the bulkhead, then Mary, then Kathleen. The two O'Malley sisters slept nearest the aisle.

We nearly have to turn over at the same time, Kathleen thought, raising up on one elbow. She looked over at where Connie O'Malley, the oldest of the two sisters, lay. Although Kathleen couldn't see Connie in the gloomy dark, she could hear the fluttery little gasps as the woman snored delicately from her end of the bunk. Kathleen hated being crammed between her mother and Rosie O'Malley, who rammed her sharp elbows into Kathleen's ribs half the night.

If I had Connie's place I might be able to get some sleep, Kathleen thought. But then she realized that even if she had an entire bunk to herself, she couldn't sleep any better. Not with the sounds that racked the passenger quarters from one end of the hold to the other.

No. Kathleen shook her head. *Don't think about it*.

The voyage so far had been torture. Most of the passengers, simple Irish farmers, had never been on a boat before, and seasickness kept them moaning in their berths. Kathleen didn't like the constant up-and-down motion of the ship but fortunately she didn't suffer from a queasy stomach. Maybe it was because she was so young. Her father had noted that the children were seldom affected by seasickness.

"Simple. After I've tried to turn over about seventeen times and Miss O'Malley has punched me another twenty times, it's usually morning."

He laughed, but there was no mirth in his voice.

A square of light suddenly appeared overhead as the hatch cover was lifted. A murmur stirred through the passengers, like a strong wind blowing reeds over a marshland.

Kathleen wasted no time. As soon as the mate lit the smoky lanterns, he would fire up the stove. She felt along the bottom of the bunk for her sack, pulling out the "sea-store" of oatmeal and the pot Liam had purchased in Sligo.

"Pardon me," Kathleen said to Rosie O'Malley as she hiked up her skirt and crawled over the old woman. She landed in the baggage-cluttered aisle, then quickly stepped aside. A man in the berth over theirs prepared to climb down. *You have to move fast around here,* Kathleen thought, *or else get knocked down.*

I've got to get there first, Kathleen vowed silently as she swung over a brass-cornered steamer trunk, scraping her shins on the hinges. She had to get there before all those other—

But she was too late. The small space under the hatchway ladder was already packed with women. Undaunted, Kathleen elbowed her way through the crowd, using her pot as a pusher.

Miss Rosie generously shared their breakfast with us."

"Did Mother eat?"

His face fell. "Not a bite. I'm afraid the fever's worse. I can feel the heat pouring off her. Have an oatcake, Kathleen."

She took the cake he held out but shook her head when he offered to assist her back into the berth. "I'm tired of eating and sleeping and living in that cage. I'm going up on deck."

"You know passengers aren't allowed up there," Liam warned.

"If I don't get some fresh air, I'll scream," she declared. "The worse the captain can do is pitch me overboard. At least that way I'd get a bath!"

"Kathleen!"

Without a backward glance, Kathleen fought her way through barrels and people until she reached the ladder that led to the deck.

"Hey, you!" a man called. "Get down!"

But Kathleen scrambled up the ladder, ignoring the splinters that needled her bare feet. The hatch was tightly closed as always, but she braced her body against the ladder and pushed it open. She climbed the next few steps slowly, poking her head through the hatch. A blast of cold salt air, the first she had felt in two weeks, slapped her in the face like a wet rag.

Several sailors worked nearby, but none

"Who are you?" Kathleen asked bluntly.

When he stood up, she saw he was about her height. He doffed his cap with a flourish. "Patrick Shannon. Pleased to meet you," he said in Gaelic. "I'll bet you're from County Galway, with that hair."

Kathleen absently shook back her ginger curls. "County Mayo, actually."

"Neighbors, then. Close enough," Patrick said expansively, as though discovering that they were related. "Are you journeying alone?"

"No. I came with my parents. My name is Kathleen O'Connor, by the way."

They shook hands solemnly. Then Patrick said, "My father and brothers stayed behind, but Da scraped together enough pennies to send me to Ameriky."

"America," Kathleen corrected.

"What?"

"It's America, not 'Ameriky.'"

His green eyes appraised her with new interest. "You speak English?"

Kathleen nodded. "My mother is half English. She was born in Ireland but grew up in Blackpool till she was eight. She went to school there. After her parents died, Mother came back to Ireland. She brought a book back with her — an English grammar. She believes in education and taught all of us English. And to read and write as well."

"You have a book? That you can read? What a wondrous thing," Patrick murmured.

Patrick was as good as his word. That afternoon, he came over to the O'Connors' berth.

"Got your pot ready?" he asked Kathleen, his coppery eyebrows arching over his eyes in exaggerated wings. "It's an amazing thing, but wouldn't you know, there's room at the stove now."

Kathleen hurried over. With that day's water ration stirred into a handful of oats, she cooked three bowls of hot mush. Liam ate his with relish, but Kathleen could not induce her mother to swallow a spoonful. She met her father's worried eyes and read the terrible truth: Mary O'Connor would never live to reach America.

And then she noticed her father's flushed cheeks, the sheen of perspiration beading his forehead, the unmistakable glitter in his eyes.

Fever. He had caught it, too.

"Your father told me I'd find you up here." Patrick squeezed behind the dinghy.

Kathleen sat huddled in the shadow between the rail and the lifeboat. She said nothing. Part of the cloud cover had lifted, leaving a sky streaked with varying shades of blue and gray. Depressing.

" 'Tis dangerous to keep coming up here, Kathleen. If you're caught abovedecks, Lord knows what the captain will do."

"You come up here," she returned evenly. "I had to get some air — get away from that

"The water keg has vinegar in it," Patrick put in.

"Vinegar? But why? Surely, they must know that vinegar is undrinkable. Do they hate us that much?" Her eyes were wide with alarm.

Patrick shook his head. "They probably dumped the vinegar out of our water cask, then added fresh water without washing it out. We're just cargo, don't you know? They've got our fares, and they don't give a fig if we get to America sick or well. That's why we have to look out for each other." His voice brightened. "But once we get to Ameriky — America — it'll be worth it."

"Will it?" Kathleen's voice was tinged with doubt.

"Sure, and it'll be grand! America is the land of plenty. Plenty of land, plenty of work, plenty of potatoes."

"But it won't be Ireland." Those five words brought back all of her sadness in a rush. She stared dully at the endless sea.

Patrick grew thoughtful, watching her. "There was a boy back home, wasn't there?" he guessed.

A pause, then Kathleen admitted, "Yes."

"He stayed behind with his family?"

"In a way. He . . . he died about six weeks ago. All of the Limericks died. Their landlord tore down their cottage when they couldn't pay the rent. They hung blankets over the ruined walls to keep out the cold. . . ."

"I'm sorry, lass."

"The horns are pointing west," Patrick observed, "showing us the way."

"Rory always said —" She broke off, unwilling to resurrect the old pain.

"Said what? Go on, lass. It's unnatural to keep it all inside. Tell me what your Rory used to say."

"He told me to make a wish on the new moon, then twirl three times and" — this was the hardest part — "kiss the person nearest, to seal the wish. If I didn't look at the moon till it was new again, my wish would come true. Pretty silly, isn't it?"

"Not at all. I'll bet if he were watching he'd want you to wish on that new moon."

"Oh, Patrick —"

"Make a wish," he prompted. "Do it for Rory. And yourself."

With a sigh, Kathleen closed her eyes, trying to summon forth a wish. But there was no hope in her heart, only the hollow space where her love for Rory Limerick had been. What was there to wish for? What did she have to look forward to in America, a strange land? Without Rory, without the familiar green hills enfolding her, she might as well be dead.

"Must be a long wish," Patrick said.

To please him, she decided to twirl on the first thought that flew in her head. *I wish to find love.* The notion shocked her. After Rory died, she knew she'd never love again. But Patrick was watching, so she spun the requi-

Chapter Three

IN the hazy, endless hours before the lamps were lit one morning, the rocking motion of the ship lulled Kathleen into uncovering memories of Rory. Two summers ago, he had taken her to the Puck Fair outside of Ballinrobe.

It was in August, 1845, the first year of the potato blight. When Rory pulled up before the O'Connor cottage in a borrowed cart pulled by a pony, Kathleen was astonished.

"Come to the fair with me," he called.

Mary O'Connor nodded her permission, and Kathleen flew out the door without even tying back her hair.

"Are you sure it's all right?" Kathleen asked Rory, climbing into the cart she knew belonged to his older brother.

"Orin said we should get out a little and have fun," Rory replied. "The potatoes are

crusty meat pies. They laughed at a puppet show, and Kathleen cheered Rory on in a foot-race even though he lost.

"I have a few pennies left over," he said when it was time to go. "What would you like?"

"Oh, Rory. You'd better save your money."

"Nonsense. I worked all summer to earn this. Are you going to deprive me of the pleasure of buying my girl a present?"

Kathleen smiled. No matter how poor Rory might be, she should have known he'd never let her leave without a trinket.

"You choose," she said at last.

He returned with a bright green ribbon trailing from his fingers. "For my lady," he said gallantly. "Such pretty hair deserves a pretty ribbon."

Kathleen flushed, then said shyly, "Will you tie it for me?"

He lifted her heavy ginger curls, gently weaving the ribbon into a wide bow. "You really *are* the prettiest girl here today."

In front of King Puck and all of Ireland, it seemed, Rory gave Kathleen her first kiss — touching her lips lightly with his. All the way home, Kathleen sat next to him in a daze. He had kissed her! From that moment on, she loved him with all her heart.

Tears slid down Kathleen's cheeks as she lay in the darkness. The next year, when the potato blight struck even more fiercely, there was no Puck Fair. The bright green ribbon faded and frayed. Rory died. Other memories

scarcely knew what the term meant anymore. How many weeks — *months* — since she last had a full stomach? "Well, I've got plenty of putrid meat, if that's what you mean. The crew brings us that horrible fish that might have been fresh three months ago."

"Some people eat it, anyway," Patrick said. "It's either that or starve."

Everything was bad and getting worse, but she couldn't lie around thinking about it. Her father needed cool cloths on his hot forehead. She saved water from her own rations to let him wet his cracked lips a few times a day. There were times when she was so thirsty, every fiber and nerve in her body screamed for water, and she had to fight back the urge to run up the ladder and fling herself overboard. When water became more precious than molten gold, Patrick rescued them from resorting to drinking stagnant sea water pooled on the floor, as many passengers were doing.

With the magic of the leprechaun he resembled, Patrick went abovedecks almost every day and smuggled down sea biscuits, fresh water and, once, a little beef jerky.

Kathleen was grateful. She cut the beef into tiny bites and fed them to her father, who had been seriously ill since the day her mother had been buried. "Say a prayer for me," he had begged Kathleen, clutching her hand. But Kathleen was glad he had not been there to witness his wife's sheet-wrapped body tossed unceremoniously over the rail.

37

ruary 7, that much she knew. Four weeks later, give or take a day, Mary O'Connor had died. Liam became ill right after, another four weeks ago. That made eight weeks, roughly. How much longer till they reached New York? When the O'Connors were given their fares to America, Lord Wyndham's agent told them that the voyage would be short — only about thirty days. But two months had passed, and no land had ever been reported.

Rosie O'Malley leaned over to tap Kathleen's leg. "Your father looks much worse today, dearie. In fact, he had a choking spell before. I thought he was ready to leave us."

Kathleen couldn't stand anymore. Excusing herself, she left the bunk.

Patrick was not in the berth he shared with four other men. Kathleen took a chance and climbed abovedecks. She found him in their usual spot, behind the lifeboat where they had first met. It had become their special meeting place. Kathleen gave him English lessons there, away from the noise and distraction of steerage. And Patrick told Kathleen stories when he sensed she was down.

"I thought you were resting," Patrick said when he saw her.

Kathleen breathed the cold salt air deeply. "I couldn't bear it down there. This is the first fresh air I've had in about four days." She gazed out over the choppy gray ocean. No sign of land, but the skies were heavy and forbidding. Seabirds struggled to stay aloft

the ocean is ice-locked this time of year," Patrick added.

"Ice? Suppose we hit some ice? Wouldn't our ship sink?"

Patrick avoided her eyes. "Sure, and it would sink like a millstone. I've looked over this ship — seen the rotten rigging. Hull's not too sound, either."

Kathleen could not bear to think about a shipwreck. Her mind just could not comprehend their boat sinking, people swimming in that frigid water.

Patrick sensed this and tactfully changed the subject. "Did you bring the book?"

"No, sorry. I left in such a hurry, I forgot. If you want another lesson, we could practice those verbs that gave you so much trouble last time."

Patrick winced. " 'Is, are, have, has.' Who can keep them straight?"

Kathleen laughed. "You've got your 'to be' verbs mixed up with the 'have' verbs."

"I'm not surprised. Tell me about America," he said. "In English. I want to see how much I've learned."

Kathleen leaned back against the dinghy. "I don't know that much about America. Only that . . . that I don't want to go."

"But it's such a grand place," Patrick protested. "I can't wait to get there. First thing I'm going to do is get a job. I'm good at cutting peat, raising potatoes."

"Do they do those things in New York?"

He stared at her. "What else can they do?

Her father drew a labored breath. His reply was barely audible. "Aye."

"Da . . ." Kathleen held his hand, almost wincing at the hot, dry flesh. Her throat tightened.

"Katie . . ." Liam waved his other hand feebly.

She bent over him to catch the faint words. ". . . the sod."

"What? Oh, the sod. What about it, Da?"

"You won't forget . . . ?"

She glanced at the sack at the foot of the bunk — the one that contained dirt that Liam had scraped from the doorway of their hut before they left their home. "Yes, Da. I'll empty the sack in America. Just as you had planned." No use pretending now. Liam O'Connor would never see New York.

". . . one . . . more . . . thing." Even though his voice was weak, Liam's accent was as familiar as the green hills of home, the lilting tone, the way each word was spoken with music and respect.

Tears trembled on Kathleen's lashes, then spilled down her cheeks. "Yes, Da?"

"You'll . . . do fine in America . . ." He paused so long, she thought he was finished. "Make your mother . . . and me proud. And . . . Katie . . . this will be hard for you . . . don't forget the magic, lass."

"I won't," she promised, crying openly now.

And then Liam gave a small sigh, like a rowan tree yielding before a strong breeze,

few grains of oatmeal and sea water. When the ship lurched, Kathleen's pot tipped over, spilling hot mush. Before she had time to react, the hatch was flung open. Two sailors scrambled down the ladder. One ran over to the stove and tossed a bucket of water over the grate, sending up a hissing cloud of steam. The women who were cooking or waiting their turn fell back, coughing and crying out. Hot cereal spattered Kathleen's skirt and scalding water droplets sprayed her bare legs. She jumped in pain, stumbling into the sailor who had thrown the water.

Tears stinging her eyes, she demanded, "What did you do that for? It's not time yet." Normally, the coals were doused at seven in the evening.

"Storm," the sailor replied curtly. "Can't take chances on fire." He raised his voice so the rest of the passengers could hear him. "No candles. Captain's orders."

At that moment the other crew member put out the last of the three lanterns, and the hold was left in semidarkness. A feeble shaft of light slanted down the open hatchway. Kathleen caught a glimpse of angry black clouds overhead.

A storm! She remembered Patrick's warning — the ship was old and falling apart. Could it withstand a storm or would they sink like a stone, as Patrick predicted?

"Is it going to be bad?" she asked the sailor anxiously.

"Bad enough." Then the two men scurried

guided her through the clutter of strewn baggage.

Kathleen crawled into her berth, aware that the O'Malley ladies were huddled against the bulkhead. "It can't last too long," she reassured them.

But it did.

Hour after hour the wind roared like a wounded dragon while the sea churned and foamed around them. The *Griffin* was tossed like a cork.

After the first few hours, the passengers, many of them already ill, began to get seasick. When the ship first set sail, Kathleen was one of the fortunate few who did not succumb to seasickness. But now the situation was different. No one able to draw breath escaped the dreaded sickness.

The ship wallowed in the gale, lifted high on a wave, then dropped down into the trough with a sickening lurch. The hull creaked and groaned as if it would break apart any second. Boxes and barrels rolled from one side of the ship to the other.

Another age passed and then the tossing began to subside. Later that day, the hatch was pried open, emitting a cold, gray light that dazzled Kathleen's eyes. Members of the crew descended the ladder and began checking the passengers. The dead were bundled and carried abovedecks while the living, who looked ghostly in the pale light, were given a water-logged biscuit and a sip of sea water.

Kathleen sat up gingerly, not certain which

Chapter Four

PATRICK forced his way through the tangle of excited passengers who were scrambling to find their baggage, his face lit by a broad grin.

Kathleen lurched from her berth to meet him. "Patrick, where are we?"

"Lass, it's the best news — we've landed in Boston!"

"Boston? Where's that? Why aren't we in New York?" Kathleen felt as though her world had been turned upside down. She only knew one town in America, and that was New York. Her father used to chant the city's name over and over during those last days of his illness, like an incantation. "When we get to New York," he'd tell Kathleen and her mother on that long walk to Sligo, "everything will be grand again."

Only the boat had not landed in New York

to set foot in the strange new world. The *Griffin* was their last link with Ireland.

The captain held his trumpet to his lips and bellowed orders for all passengers to disembark immediately or they'd be tossed overboard. Kathleen looked around for Patrick. He had helped her up the ladder and at the top handed her the two sacks. She thought he was right behind her. Where was he?

A bearded sailor, seeing her hesitation, took her elbow and steered her into the crowd. Kathleen was swept down the gangplank, caught in the tide of alarmed immigrants. At the bottom of the plank, several passengers dumped sacks of sod onto the pier, then bent and kissed the earth.

Kathleen felt the weight of Liam's sack. She turned the bag upside down, emptying the contents, then uttered a brief prayer. "I made it, Da. I'm in America."

That done, she looked around for Patrick. Was he still on board? The way the crew was pitching luggage over the rail and herding passengers down the plank, it seemed unlikely.

She wandered down the wharf, goggle-eyed at the hordes of people bumping into her, pushing, yelling — more people than she had thought lived in the world. Boston must be a huge place! A man slammed into her, hard enough to bruise her shoulder.

"Watch where you're walking, sister!"

Kathleen mumbled an apology, appalled at

nearby on his steamer trunk, obviously unsure of what to do next. She was about to ask him if he had seen Patrick, when a big boy thundered up the wharf, knocked the man off his trunk, then shouldered the baggage and ran away, calling, "Follow me to Rosie Donegal's boardinghouse!"

What kind of place *was* this America?

A line of people were being driven by an official-looking man wielding a nightstick toward an enormous building of forbidding granite blocks. Another man stood along one side of the wharf, bawling, "All immigrants must go through customs. All immigrants must go through customs."

Kathleen felt a jab of panic. Customs? What was that? She didn't want to go into that bleak-looking building. What would they do to her, especially once they found out that her parents had died on the voyage and she was alone? Suppose there was a rule that said young girls could not stay in America without their parents?

Where was Patrick? He had promised to help her!

Abruptly, Kathleen turned away from the immigrants marching dolefully toward the customs building, their rain-drenched clothes flapping in the wind. She drew her blanket-shawl over her bright hair, hoping she didn't look too Irish. Then she fished her wooden clogs out of her sack and put them on. People in America did not go barefoot.

She needed help, but who could she turn

plenty, she thought grimly, you'd never know it by this waterfront. No matter. Even if America was ten times worse than the ship, Kathleen would not let it get her down. After all, she was an O'Connor — a family as old as Ireland itself, her father used to remark with pride. She had promised him she would make it in America. And she would — *without* Patrick Shannon's help.

"You look like a determined girl." A smooth voice suddenly cut into her musings. The accent was curiously flat, with all the consonants hard-edged. The speaker moved into her line of vision. He was a young man, only a few years older than she was, wearing a soiled frock coat several sizes too large, dirty trousers, and cracked boots. The brim of his slouch cap was pulled low over his face, but Kathleen made out a pointed, foxy chin and narrow eyes under beetle brows.

"Are you speaking to me?" she asked warily.

"Yes, indeed." The boy advanced a few steps, his shoulders hunched against the bone-chilling rain. "I've been watching you. You handle yourself pretty well for a greenie."

"A what?"

"Greenie. Short for greenhorn."

"What's that?" It didn't sound flattering, whatever it was.

"Never mind. I saw you slip past the customs agent. And a few minutes ago, you sidestepped that policeman back there."

cept handouts like a gypsy tinker, but she was too hungry to worry about that now. She snatched the crust eagerly, watching the boy's face as she ate.

"The name's Dick Whistle. What's yours?"

"Kathleen O'Connor."

"All right, Kathleen," Dick said companionably. "You work for me and I'll give you two percent of the take. Plus meals and board. If you're any good, I'll up your take to five percent."

Even though he spoke English, Kathleen understood very little of Dick's conversation. What on earth was "take"? But she managed to figure out that she would be fed and would not have to sleep on the docks. "What do I have to do?"

"Pick pockets."

Her jaw dropped. "You mean steal?"

"That's right." Dick never batted an eyelash. He was as calm as though they were discussing the weather.

A ponderous silence hung between them, marked by the *split-splat* of rain dripping off the eaves of a nearby warehouse. Kathleen thought over his offer. Food. And bed. And possibly a little money. The alternative? She glanced back at the rain-soaked tents. Without money, life in America could be very harsh. But would she steal to stay alive? Yes, she would.

"I'll do it," she told him.

He broke into a triumphant grin. "Fine! You won't be sorry. Now, let's get along to

Dick Whistle had been true to his word. Mrs. McCracken was not exactly a saint, but she ran an honest boardinghouse, even if the meals were a little skimpy. Kathleen shared a bed with two other girls, both younger than she. The sheets were made of the coarsest cambric but were reasonably clean.

After work, everyone threw that day's "take" on the big table. Dick divided the money evenly between himself and Mrs. McCracken. He took the other stolen goods like pocketbooks, watches, jewelry, and handkerchiefs to sell. At the end of the week, the "workers" each received their share.

Kathleen's compact size and catlike agility worked to her advantage. She proved to be an excellent pickpocket. After a few practice sessions, Dick took her back down to the docks. There he bumped into unwary passengers, apologizing profusely, often tripping the person again. Meanwhile, Kathleen would search the victim's pockets, taking whatever she could.

"I won't steal from Irish people," Kathleen declared that first morning.

"But Kathleen, lass," Dick wheedled. "All the ships pouring into Boston harbor are loaded with Irish!"

"I don't care. It would be like stealing from . . . my own parents, God rest their souls."

Dick sighed, giving in. "The Irish don't have anything worth stealing, anyway."

"It's very pretty." Kathleen looked down at Jimmy's tousled brown hair. A cowlick sprang up in an endearing clump. *Such a nice little boy, what a shame he has to be out on the streets at his age,* she thought. Orphaned at the age of six, Jimmy had no home other than Mrs. McCracken's. And the wharfs.

"There's a ship dockin' now," Jimmy said, pointing to a *Griffin*-sized vessel nuzzling into the slip. "Who's trippin' first?" he asked as they waited for the gangplank to be lowered. Passengers lining the deck leaned eagerly over the rail.

"You bump," Kathleen replied. She preferred to do the stealing as much as possible, since Jimmy was so young. That way, if she was caught, he had a chance to get away.

Immigrants hurled down the plank, stopping in confusion when they stepped onto the pier, just as she had done two weeks ago. Jimmy sidled up to a man with ginger whiskers.

Kathleen grabbed his arm. "Not him. He's Irish. That fat one over there. With that potbelly, I'm sure he's English."

Jimmy worked his way through the crowd, like a salmon swimming upstream, until he was close to the fat man. Kathleen maneuvered herself until she was behind the victim. Jimmy began to cry, an act he had perfected under Dick Whistle's coaching.

"Mama! Mama!" he sobbed, his thin shoulders heaving, a fist scrubbing at one eye, the very picture of a child who had lost

nor." When Jimmy had left, Patrick turned to her. "When I heard about this red-haired female pickpocket, I had a feeling it might be you. For heaven's sake, Kathleen!"

"But Patrick —"

"We won't talk about it now. The important thing is, I've found you. Kathleen, I been worried sick these last few weeks. I thought I'd lost you forever!"

He sat down and gripped her hands. "Are you all right? Have you been mistreated? Because if you have, I —"

"I'm fine, Patrick. And so glad to see you! Tell me how you found me."

"In a second," he replied impatiently. "Guess what? I've got a job — and one for you, too! Honest work, not stealing."

"A real job?" Kathleen's eyes widened. "Oh, Patrick, that's wonderful. Where?"

"At this grand house. The Thornleys are so rich, it makes me giddy to imagine all their money!"

Rich people. Suddenly Kathleen remembered Lord Wyndham, their landlord, who lived in his fancy Grimsby Hall. An arrogant man, Lord Wyndham showed no more concern for his Irish tenants than a basket of unwanted kittens. When he evicted her family, she vowed she would despise rich people till the day she died, and never have anything to do with them.

And now she was going to work for a wealthy family.

could get a job that day, and then I'd come back here in the evening to look for you. But getting work wasn't that easy. They don't cut peat here, I found. There are so many trees, people burn firewood. Imagine. And I couldn't find a potato patch anywhere, though I walked till my feet gave out."

"But you did find a job . . . and one for me, too?"

Patrick's face lighted. "At the finest place you ever set eyes on, Kathleen! I work in the stables, taking care of eight darlin' horses."

"That's nice." She knew he loved horses, like many Irish boys. "What about me? What do I do?"

"You've got the best job of all. Working in the house, Kathleen. Right in the kitchen! You can eat all you please."

Kathleen, who had not ventured beyond the waterfront since landing in Boston, was gawking at the sights around her. Warehouses and taverns had given way to more refined tea shops and stores. People dressed in rich clothes rode smart carriages through neat, brick-paved streets. A young woman, not much older than Kathleen, wearing a silk gown splashed with turquoise flowers, drove a red-painted pony trap, bright as a tinker's wagon, her gloved hands expertly handling the reins. A large carriage driven by a liveried coachman passed by, giving Kathleen an envious glimpse of velvet cloaks and beribboned bonnets. The coachman's burgundy jacket matched the carriage robes the

sunshine. Delicate, wrought-iron handrails curled out from the porches.

"What huge houses Americans have," Kathleen marveled.

"Those aren't all one house," Patrick explained. "Watkins — he's the groom I work for — told me they are called row houses. Each family lives in a different section. Sort of like stalls, only for people."

Even at that, Kathleen decided, tilting her head back to take in all three stories, Americans must be awfully rich to have all that space. The cottage back home had only one room, plus a cramped sleeping loft. *Back home* . . . She had to stop thinking that way. The hut was gone, and everything she had ever known was lost forever.

Then she saw a white placard in the window of a millinery shop: HELP WANTED — NO IRISH. She grabbed Patrick's arm. "What does that sign mean? It says 'Help Wanted — No —' "

"I know what it says." Patrick sighed. "It means exactly what it says. The people offering the position don't want Irish to apply."

"But why? What's wrong with us?"

"We're Irish . . . and we're Catholic. That's what one man told me. When I was looking for work, I kept seeing those signs all over town, but since I can't read, I'd go in and ask about a job, anyway. Now I know what those letters spell," he added dourly.

But he still hadn't answered her question. "What's wrong with being Irish in this coun-

everyone in Boston, except the Irish, was wealthy. But as nice as the houses were, she found the scene curiously strange. She missed the rolling green moors of Ireland, the still waters of Lake Maske, the cozy thatch-roofed huts. Here, all was brick and granite. And the noise! Carriages clattering over the cobblestones, pushcart vendors calling to advertise their wares. Back home, the only sounds she remembered were Mr. Mac-Gowan's sheep bleating on the hill behind their cottage and the wind sighing through the glen.

"That's it," Patrick said suddenly, his voice throbbing with excitement. "That's the Thornley house."

Kathleen turned, expecting to see another row of town houses. Instead, a sweep of magnificent lawn, encased in what seemed to be miles of spear-topped wrought-iron fencing, met her startled eyes. Set well back from the street, showcased like a rare carving on a drape of green velvet, was the Thornley house.

House, Kathleen thought, eyes widening with awe, *is too ordinary a word to describe such a wonderful place. Palace, maybe. Or mansion. But never just house.*

The Thornley estate covered the entire block; the house sprawled lazily over most of the shamrock-green lawn, guarded by straight-backed elms and silver-barked maples just beginning to bud. Time had mellowed the red brick facade to a soft peach.

and gaze at the violet fanlight over the door.

But Patrick was leading her around the back, down a flagstone path bordered by deep boxwood hedges. "We have to use the servant's entry. Remember that, Kathleen. Never go up to the front door. The butler told me that."

After the splendor of the front entrance, the servant's entry was a dissappointment — just a plain wooden door with a bell next to the handle. As much as Kathleen craved to go through those magnificent doors, she refused to let a little thing like this burst her bubble of excitement. Then she remembered her promise — how had she forgotten so quickly? No matter how wonderful the Thornleys were, no matter how lovely their house, they were still rich people, and that made them the enemy. Because of their wealth, they were somehow distantly related to Lord Wyndham in Kathleen's mind. She knew she'd despise them without a shred of remorse.

Patrick rang the bell. Kathleen's stomach knotted with apprehension. She felt very bedraggled suddenly, conscious of her uncombed hair and grimy, torn woolen dress.

"Do I look all right?" she whispered urgently.

He looked at her. "Pretty as an Irish sunset," he replied, and meant it.

The door opened and a tall girl with straw-colored hair tucked under a ruffled white cap thrust a surly face out into the sun.

one wall, large enough to accommodate eight-foot logs. An ox could be roasted with no difficulty. A cauldron swinging from a crane simmered above the licking flames. Over the fireplace were two ovens, and a woodstove stood nearby.

An open-shelved Welsh cupboard, painted buttermilk green, took up the entire wall opposite the bank of windows. White iron-stone serving platters and bowls, in all shapes and sizes, leaned against the slender rails. Kathleen thought she had never seen anything so beautiful as the sight of all those round and oval platters shining against the rich green-painted wood.

"Did you turn to stone or something?" The girl Patrick had called Tessie frowned at her. "Don't just stand there. Cook wants you."

A round, dumpling-shaped woman came out of a room just beyond the serving cupboard. She wiped her hands on the voluminous apron that swathed her bulky form. Her red cheeks looked cheery, but the blue eyes that appraised Kathleen were sharp.

"Here's the new girl, Cook," Tessie announced, not bothering to conceal her displeasure.

"This her?" Cook waddled over, looking Kathleen up and down. "Too skinny, but then they all are. When was the last time you ate? Never mind, what's your name?"

"Uh — Kathleen O'Connor." She watched the big woman move toward the cupboard

enough. I believe you. Good for you, Kathleen O'Connor. Your mother must be quite a woman."

"She was," Kathleen said, her voice low. "She died on the boat coming over. And my father."

"So you're all alone," Cook said. "Tess, hurry up with that food. Sit down, Kathleen." She yanked a stool from under the worktable.

Ungraciously, Tess set down a dish of dark-red beans, accompanied by a round of moist, brown bread.

Kathleen stared at the meal before her. The bowl was thick white china, so different from the cheap crockery she was used to. She fingered the fine pewter spoon. The food looked so strange, she hesitated, despite her hunger. But Cook and Tessie were watching her, so she picked up the spoon and began to eat.

The beans had a peculiar, tangy taste she would later learn was due to molasses and salt pork, and the steamed bread was hearty, sweetened with sour milk and raisins. But the flavors were odd, unfamiliar. Kathleen longed for her mother's colcannon, a combination of mashed potatoes and cabbage, accompanied by a slab of soda bread.

"All right," Cook said when Kathleen had cleaned her dish. "Time to get busy. Tess, take Kathleen into the scullery and start her on the vegetables."

She contemplated the pile of vegetables on the knife-scarred table, still dirty from being dug out of the root cellar. If there was one thing she could do well, it was peel potatoes. She chose a paring knife from the rack on the wall, then got to work.

Thirty minutes later, the swill basket at her feet was filled with neat potato parings and carrot scrapings. She gathered the vegetables in a pan and went back into the kitchen. Cook was stirring the pot of beans, steaming-hot from the oven.

"Done already?" she said, noting the cleaned vegetables with surprise. "Set them down there. Master David likes potatoes and carrots with his beans and bread. Been fixing them for him for nigh onto eighteen years now."

As she worked, Cook told Kathleen that the Thornleys, like many Boston families, had baked beans and brown bread for supper every Saturday. It was an easy meal for Cook, since the beans simmered all day, freeing her to prepare ahead for the big Sunday dinner. She seemed to enjoy talking to Kathleen.

Then Tessie came in and stared pointedly at the flagstone floor. Kathleen fetched the pail and mop from the scullery and swabbed the floor until the smooth slate stones shone like ebony. By then it was time to serve supper.

"The Family always eats early on Saturday," Cook remarked. The way she referred

that much food. What happened to the rest?

As if reading her thoughts, Cook said, "Don't worry. There'll be plenty left for us. The servants eat in here, after the Family is through. Except for Brooks and Miss Devon. Tess will take trays to their rooms."

So many names — would she ever get them all straight? The Thornleys must employ a lot of people. Suddenly, the difference between the world Kathleen had grown up in and this house loomed before her, as vast and boundless as the ocean she had crossed to get here. Did she really belong in this house?

Later, Tessie and Kathleen washed the dishes while Cook sat in the rocking chair by the fire, her feet on a stool, sipping tea.

Kathleen tried to make conversation. "Have you worked here long?"

"Long enough." Tessie pointed at the kettle Kathleen was scrubbing. "That's not clean. You probably don't wash pots so good in Ireland, but here we're pretty particular." She inspected the pan Kathleen rewashed. "That's why they let me serve. The missus wants a girl who'll do it properly, get the courses straight. And know what each person likes. Now, Master David, he wants a lot of gravy on his potatoes, but Miss Victoria only takes a dab."

"It sounds interesting," Kathleen said.

"For sure *you'll* never be asked to serve or do anything where the Family will see you," Tessie said haughtily.

Kathleen was about to take exception to

Chapter Six

AT five in the morning, the kitchen was as chilly and drafty as a medieval castle in midwinter.

Kathleen clumped across the stone floor in her wood clogs, wishing she had a pair of trim leather boots like those Tessie wore. She went over to the wood box next to the fireplace and took out several sticks. With the iron poker, she stirred the banked embers before laying the kindling across the grate.

The day before, Cook had outlined Kathleen's duties. "Every morning you'll get up first to lay the fires. Every second day, the grates must be cleaned, the ashed raked out, and the andirons black-leaded. You will also heat and carry water. Besides helping me prepare food, you'll keep the kitchen, pantry, and scullery clean. You have Thursday and Sunday evenings off and Sunday mornings to go to church."

much to do, you know, except fetch and carry for the missus and Miss Victoria."

Kathleen's head fairly spun at all the names and positions. From Tessie's tone, she gathered that "the missus" was Mrs. Thornley. Victoria was the daughter. And David the son. But so many servants! Upstairs maids, downstairs maids, butlers, governesses . . . Didn't rich people do *anything* for themselves?

"Here we are," Tessie said when they reached the top of the stairs. She opened the first door on the right off a bare, dimly lit hallway.

Kathleen stepped inside hesitantly, clutching her sack. Four narrow beds, one in each corner, filled the tiny room. Tucked between deep dormer windows was an oak washstand, the only other piece of furniture. Still, this room was better furnished than any place Kathleen had lived before.

"That's your bed." Tessie pointed to an iron bedstead topped by a straw mattress. A coarse brown blanket lay folded at the foot.

A plump brown-haired girl was pouring water from a stoneware pitcher into a matching bowl. Her eyes widened with curiosity at Kathleen. "Who's this?" she asked.

"New scullery girl," Tessie said bluntly. "Cook hired her today."

"Irish," Emma said. It was a statement, not a question. Her voice was as flat and unmusical as Tessie's, Kathleen noted. "Does she understand English?"

end of the world? And why did her parents have to die? If they were still alive, no doubt Kathleen's life would be different. It would be a struggle here, to be sure, but at least they'd have each other.

Thank heaven for Patrick, Kathleen thought. He worked and lived in the stables, so she probably wouldn't see him often. But the knowledge that he was near reassured her.

Emma finished washing, and dried her face on a towel. "There's a box under the bed," she said to Kathleen, "to put your things in."

"I don't have much." Kathleen took the English grammar out of her sack. "Only this." She smoothed the worn leather cover. How many times had Mary O'Connor opened that book, long, slender fingers lingering over the marble-printed end papers, before turning the pages carefully to that day's lesson?

"A book?" Emma stared at it, puzzled. "That's all you have? Just a book?"

"She can *read,*" Tessie put in, coming down emphatically on the last word.

"Really?" Emma turned back to look at Kathleen in astonishment, as though her face had suddenly turned green.

Tessie took the pins from her hair, shaking the sparse strands into a fan across her shoulders. "Yes, indeed. Didn't you know the Thornleys are hiring high-quality scullery girls these days? Educated, yet!"

She sat down on the stool, her shoulders slumped with despair, putting her chin in her hands.

A ginger-striped cat wandered into the kitchen, undoubtedly seeking a warm hearth. The cat came over to Kathleen and rubbed against her ankles.

"Hello, kitty." She reached down to stroke the burnished fur. "You lonely, too?"

The cat rubbed back and forth, stopping once or twice to give Kathleen's ankle a tiny nip. She loved animals, remembering how sad she had been whenever she saw starved cats and dogs lying along the road from her village to Sligo.

She bent to pick up the cat, a little startled at the animal's solid weight.

"You're heavier than you look," she said, tucking the cat's head under her chin. She walked over to the fire, so that they both could bask in the heat for a few minutes. The cat purred in her arms, completely content. Kathleen gazed into the leaping yellow-and-orange flames, burning blue close to the center. *Rory's eyes were that shade,* she mused, then abruptly dismissed the thought. Would everything blue remind her of him? Would every blackbird flying overhead make her recall his raven-wing hair? Would every endless night remind her how empty her life was without him?

"Are you real?" a reedy voice said at her elbow.

Kathleen turned to see a little girl about

she replied, her voice taut with caution. "I thought so! No wonder you're so pretty. Do you know any stories? My papa says all Irish are full of stories — they'd rather talk than work!"

Looking at the child's homely face, Kathleen decided that Pippa was merely parroting something she had heard without realizing what it meant. Handing the heavy cat to Pippa, Kathleen said, "My father told me lots of stories when I was your age. Mostly about fairies. Do you like fairies?"

"I love them. I'm always looking for them, but Victoria says only babies believe in fairies and there really aren't any. Is that true?" she asked, stroking the cat she cradled in her arms.

"My father always said that no one had ever proved that there *weren't* any Little People, and until then, he would believe what he pleased."

Pippa draped the cat over her shoulders where he lay limply, like a fur cape. "Will you tell me a story now?"

Kathleen glanced nervously out the window. Faint streaks of ivory lightened the sky. Cook would be down any minute to start breakfast. If she saw Kathleen idling with Pippa, she'd probably be angry.

"I can't right now," she said, hoping the child would take the hint and leave. "I have work to do."

"I'll help," Pippa offered. "Patrick let me polish the horse brasses yesterday. Have you

rice and meal, all full to the brim; muslin-wrapped loaves of salt and sugar; crocks of molasses, dried beans, and preserves. Outside, Cook showed her the potatoes, carrots, and onions buried in the root cellar. Butter, milk, and cream were stored in the buttery. The ice house provided ice for cold summertime drinks and frozen desserts.

Today was Sunday. Kathleen knew that Cook planned an after-church feast that would make last night's supper seem paltry. So much food. Why not feed the cat mackerel and cream?

Kathleen turned from her work to look at Pippa Thornley, who was rearranging the spoons and spatulas on the table into a geometric pattern. She was a plain child, with lank, mud-brown hair straggling down her back. Her nose was too big and her teeth were crooked. But she had warm brown eyes, and her smile was engaging.

She can't help it she's plain, Kathleen thought. Still, she couldn't help but compare this little girl to her own sisters. Kerry, who had had curly copper hair and heather-green eyes and could dance the liveiest jig in three counties, and dreamed of dancing at Dublin Castle. And Meara, the baby. Dark-haired and blue-eyed, a fairy changeling in a family of red hair and green eyes. Meara had laughed and squealed, and was adored by all the O'Connors. Such spirited, pretty girls, as full of promise as new candles. But then the famine came and their flames were doused

not Pippa's fault that she's rich. And she could scarcely be blamed for thousands starving in far-off countries.

"Pippa Thornley! Did you sneak down the back stairs again?"

Kathleen whirled from the worktable to see her second early-morning visitor. Her first thought, she remembered later, was ridiculous: *David Thornley is much better-looking from the front than he is from the back.*

The tantalizing glimpse of David on the stair landing the night before had left her curious. Now, seeing him face-to-face like this, she felt shaken from head to foot, as though all the ancient powers from the standing stones at Carrowaglogh reverberated through her.

But David did not even notice her. He came into the kitchen, dressed in cream-colored trousers and a soft green flannel shirt, open at the throat.

"What are you doing here?" he chided his little sister, running an exasperated hand through unruly peat-brown hair. Kathleen noted that the hair curling around his ears and forehead was an even lighter shade of brown, nearly gold. "When Miss Devon gets up, she'll be mad as a scalded cat if she finds you gone again."

"She won't be up for hours," Pippa sniffed. "And don't talk about scalded cats in front of Oliver. It upsets him. Anyway, Miss Devon snores so loud, I couldn't sleep. And

and led her out of the kitchen. Kathleen stared at the closed door. Next to Rory, David Thornley was the handsomest boy she had ever seen. No, just as good-looking as Rory but in a different way. Where Rory's lean jaw and ink-black hair reminded Kathleen of the old Irish kings, David's face was honest and open, almost like a child's. But there was nothing childish about the way he had looked at her.

Did he look at all girls that way? she wondered. What *was* there about him? And then she knew —David Thornley did not give her that "Oh, you're Irish" look she had come to recognize and hate. His smile was genuine, and when Pippa had called attention to Kathleen's hair, his face lit up appreciatively. Did he really think she was pretty, even in this awful dress? Of course, he said she was prettier than Pippa's cat — not quite the same thing. . . .

The door thumped open again and Cook came in, tying the big white apron over her work dress.

"Morning, Kathleen. You've got a good fire going, I see. The girl before you couldn't start a decent fire if lightning struck the fireplace." She nodded at the cutlery and serving dishes laid out on the table. "Exactly what I need this morning. You're doing just fine, Kathleen."

Tessie ran in then, tucking wisps of hair into her cap.

"You're late," Cook accused.

bother. If you want something done right, you have to do it yourself." She brushed past Kathleen.

Tessie walked by, carrying the kettle of hot water. The triumphant smirk on her face told Kathleen everything. Tessie deliberately misled her. And now Cook, who had been showing signs of liking her, was angry.

I'm just the Irish girl to them, she thought. *Worth nothing. And nothing I do will ever change that.*

was good, Tessie visited her parents' farm in Haverhill, a town outside of Boston. Kathleen knew that Tessie gave part of her salary to her struggling family. Once, Kathleen asked Tessie if she minded being so far from home.

"Not a whit," the other girl replied smartly. "An hour a week there is enough. I'm only too glad to get back here."

Kathleen was shocked. "How can you say that? If you don't have anything else in this world, you have your family." Now, more than ever, she realized how much she missed her parents. "At least you can go back to the house you grew up in —"

"And couldn't wait to get away from," Tessie finished. "You don't seem to understand, new girl. There is nothing there for me, except marriage to some old geezer who would work me like a mule on his poor farm. No, thanks. I had enough hardship growing up. Poppa tried, but we never seemed to have any money. There's seven in our family, and the only clothes I ever owned were handed down from two older sisters."

Hand-me-down clothes a hardship? Is that *all*? Kathleen refrained from letting Tessie know what *real* hardships were: famine, leaving home to go live in a foreign country, watching loved ones die. . . .

"I intend to make something of my life," Tessie went on. "I don't want to end up like my mother and sisters. Every week, when I go home, I see what would be in store for me

kitchen since that first morning when Pippa, and then David, surprised her. Kathleen didn't care — one day was like another, and as long as she kept busy, her thoughts didn't stray to Ireland, or her parents . . . or Rory.

On May Day morning, though, Kathleen paused as she filled the water pails. May Day. She and her sister Kerry used to celebrate by strewing primrose petals over the doorsills of close neighbors. But May Day in America was evidently just another day.

Cook approached Kathleen, her round face clearly agitated. "Tessie has a nasty cold. She could barely serve breakfast without sneezing in the bacon. I sent her back to bed. She's not fit for work today."

"She coughed and sneezed all night," Kathleen added. "And her face is flushed with fever. Will she be all right?"

"She'll live." From Cook's tone and jerky movements as she sliced lemons, Kathleen realized that the older woman's leg was flaring up again. She had learned that whenever Cook was grouchy, it was due to a painfully swollen knee. "What a day to be shorthanded. Brooks is out on an errand. And the missus is having one of her famous tea parties." Cook glanced at the clock that stood on the Welsh dresser. "Lordy me, I've got to hurry. Now, listen, Kathleen, you'll have to serve tea. Nothing to it. I'll fix the tray. All you have to do is pour and ask what they want in it."

Kathleen, who had been putting away

She knows, Kathleen thought as she ran up the back stairs. *Cook knows that Tessie doesn't like me.*

Tessie was sitting up in bed, sneezing into a big blue handkerchief. "What do you want?" she greeted sullenly, wiping gingerly at her raw, red nose.

"Cook says I have to serve tea, and I have nothing suitable to wear. She wants me to borrow your gray dress." Kathleen spilled the words in a rush, afraid she might lose her nerve.

"My gray dress!" Tessie moaned, as if Kathleen had asked for an ermine robe. "That's my second-best dress." Pulling the covers up to her chin, she nodded toward the peg rack where the girls hung their clothes. "Take it. But be *very careful.* Don't spill anything on it — gray shows spots. If you ruin it, you'll be sorry."

"I'll be careful," Kathleen promised.

The dove-gray dress was plain and serviceable, the only ornamentation a row of pearl buttons down the bodice. Kathleen stripped off her old brown wool eagerly and slipped the smooth cotton over her head. The skirt fell in a circle well below her shoe tops.

Kathleen gathered the skirt in her hands and ran back down the stairs, before Tessie changed her mind. She suspected that Tessie would never have been so generous if she hadn't been sick.

The silver tea set gleamed on its matching tray. Cook had filled the sugar bowl and

walnut front doors. Sunlight streamed through the lavender window, falling in broken patterns on the parquet floor. The crescent moon blazed in the center of the fan-shaped glass. A mirrored oak closet stood just inside the door, with hooks for visitor's cloaks and hats. Seascapes of Boston harbor in massive gilt frames hung on the opposite wall. A gateleg table held the brass lamps that Tessie filled every morning, trimming the wicks, and lit each evening. Next to a cranberry glass vase, Kathleen saw calling cards on a silver tray. Mrs. Thornley had received a lot of guests.

The grandfather clock chiming ten o'clock jolted Kathleen out of her trance, reminding her she had a job to do. Taking a deep breath, she entered the first door on the right, angling the heavy tray to fit through the door-way.

"Here she is," a voice edged with aggravation spoke. A heavyset woman in a rustling lilac satin gown came forward. She stopped when she saw Kathleen. "Who are you? Where's Tessie?" she demanded, her hooded, deep-set eyes dark with suspicion.

Under the woman's intimidating gaze, Kathleen felt her knees buckle, and she nearly dropped the tray. She recovered before the cream spilled out of the pitcher, swallowing her fear. "Tessie is sick, ma'am. I'm Kathleen — I usually work in the kitchen."

"Oh. The new scullery girl. Well, if Tessie is ill, it can't be helped. Put the tray down

dress Kathleen had ever seen. She longed to touch the soft, shiny fabric.

"Are you going to give me those tongs, or am I to reach into the bowl with my bare fingers?" the girl asked Kathleen coldly.

She handed the tongs to the girl. "I'm sorry. I — all this is new to me."

"That's evident." The girl helped herself to three lumps of sugar. Her brown eyes flickered over Kathleen, taking in the ill-fitting gray dress, red-gold curls tumbling from the white ruffled cap.

Kathleen felt an unwanted blush creep up her neck. Instinctively, she knew this was Victoria Thornley. David's sister. Her guess was confirmed when one of the women seated on the divan said, "Victoria, where *did* you get that stunning gown?"

"Would you please move?" the girl told Kathleen. "I can't see through you." Kathleen hastily stepped aside, catching the heel of her clog on the fringed edge of the Persian rug. The girl rolled her eyes heavenward. "Good help really *is* hard to find. Excuse me, Mrs. Winthrop, you were asking about my gown? Papa brought the silk back from Lyons when he was in Europe last summer. The color is called Ophelia rose — it *is* pretty, isn't it?"

"I wish my Elaine could wear that shade of pink," Mrs. Winthrop said. "It's perfect on you, Victoria, with your dark hair."

"Victoria has always known which colors flatter her best," Mrs. Thornley put in.

blue-and-white china plates and vases, and figurines in the shape of milkmaids and Chinese
dogs. A pale green vase with Greek figures
around the base held an ivy plant. Kathleen
had no idea what the names of these things
were, but she knew they were very expensive.
Taken singly, the objects were beautiful. But
Mrs. Thornley's penchant for clutter lessened
the significance of the individual pieces.

Kathleen fought a strong desire to sweep
everything off a table and display one elegant
vase.

All of Mrs. Thornley's guests wore bonnets, and all were gowned in elaborate dresses
of voile or satin. As Kathleen refilled teacups,
she noticed ruby and diamond rings on fingers, heavy gold bangles around wrists, and
sapphire-studded watch pins fastened to embroidered bodices. Did rich ladies put on
every piece of jewelry they owned to go
calling?

By contrast, Mrs. Thornley was hatless,
her stocky body encased in violet satin, a
Brussels lace collar falling over her broad
shoulders. Clearly, her daughter was the star
of this gathering, looking luminously beautiful in her pink gown, like a rose freshly
plucked from a dew-damp garden.

The women were chattering about the latest possessions they had acquired. It seemed
to Kathleen a rather tedious topic, since each
woman was required, as though by unwritten
social convention, to outdo the others.

". . . the very latest thing," Mrs. Winthrop

Mrs. Thornley ushered her guests from the room, leaving Kathleen alone. She carefully loaded the trays and was startled when Brooks came in.

"Mrs. Thornley was impressed with the way you filled in for Tessie," he said. "And Mrs. Thornley is very difficult to please."

Kathleen was surprised; she thought she had served rather clumsily.

"As a matter of fact," the butler continued, "we discussed promoting you to parlor maid — on a trial basis, of course. Cook is sorry to lose you. She had nothing but good things to say about your work."

Stunned, Kathleen let the significance of his words sink in. When she was able to speak, her voice came out a tremulous whisper. "You want *me* to be parlor maid?"

"You'll get a raise, naturally, but there will be additional responsibilities. If you think you can handle it, the position is yours."

That evening, Kathleen went up the back stairs in a daze. Parlor maid! More money! And best of all, an opportunity to look at — and touch — those lovely things.

Emma was sitting on Tessie's bed when Kathleen walked in. She got up, throwing Tessie a meaningful look.

Tessie narrowed her watery blue eyes at Kathleen. "Heard you got yourself promoted, new girl. Pretty fast work, I'd say."

"I didn't ask for the job, if that's what you think," Kathleen said defensively. "I'm just as surprised as you are."

band of her skirt, then climbed the ladder, balancing a pan of sudsy water on the top step. To her dismay, she discovered the ladder wobbled, and she had to stand on the second rung from the top in order to reach the window.

She had just cleaned the first wedge-shaped pane when the front door handle jiggled. Someone was coming in! Before she could climb down, the front door opened abruptly, jostling the unsteady ladder. Kathleen caught herself by hanging onto the ledge over the door, but couldn't prevent the pan of water from tipping.

Horrified, she watched as soapy water doused David Thornley as he came in the door.

Kathleen wished the ceiling would open and an unseen hand would reach down and scoop her up. How could she face him? What must he *think?* Worse, would she be fired for this? She could not stay on the ladder forever, much as she wanted to. Hesitantly, she backed down the rungs. A warm hand closed around her waist, steadying her as she climbed down the wobbly ladder.

When she stood on the parquet floor, David said, "There. That wasn't so bad, was it?" He touched her chin lightly. "Stop trembling. Nothing's going to happen."

"But your hair! And your coat!" Kathleen's eyes widened at the sight of his soaked wool jacket, his plastered hair. "It's all my fault! I'm so sorry —"

David shushed her. "I told you I was to blame. I barged in the door like a charging buffalo. You had no idea someone would come in."

How nice he was, taking the blame for her blunder. Did he realize she was afraid of losing her job?

"You know," David remarked, stepping back to stare down into her face, "you don't look a *thing* like Pippa's cat. Oliver always looks so smug in that way spoiled cats have. No, there's something about you. . . ." Impulsively, he reached up and pulled off her white cap. Red-gold curls spilled over her shoulders, nearly down to her waist. "You've got the kind of hair that should be worn loose and free. Not stuffed in that awful cap."

papers. That's all. Nothing important."

"But —"

"Don't bother, Kathleen. No harm done." The friendliness in his brown eyes dissolved as he stuffed the soggy envelope into his jacket. "Hello, Brooks," he greeted the white-haired butler who was coming down the hall, his face wrinkled with concern.

"What happened here?" the butler asked, giving Kathleen a long, hard glare.

"It looks worse than it really is," David said smoothly. "I bumped into Kathleen's ladder. Nearly knocked the poor girl off. I'm just glad she wasn't hurt."

Kathleen shot him a grateful look. Even now he took her side!

"Of course, Master David. You'd better get out of that wet coat," Brooks advised. He watched until David was nearly at the top of the mahogany staircase before he added in a sterner tone, "Kathleen, mop up this water immediately before it stains the floor."

"Yes, sir." She picked up the dishpan and rag. As she turned to go back down the hall, she saw a figure leaning over the rail of the gallery that looked out over the foyer.

It was David. He held the sodden envelope loosely in one hand as he stared down at Kathleen. His eyes caught hers for a moment.

Kathleen felt trapped by the intensity of his gaze, just as she'd been overwhelmed by Rory Limerick's power that long-ago after-noon on the old druid burial ground. She never dreamed that a boy could make her

ing five enormous rooms from sunup to sundown left her too tired for recreation.

Today, though, even Cook advised her to get out of the house. "You're too pale, Kathleen. Get some fresh air and let that handsome stable lad squire you around a bit."

After washing the supper dishes, Kathleen changed into the midnight-blue serge dress Cook had cut down from one of her own ample dresses, then brushed her ginger curls until they gleamed, excited at the prospect of seeing Patrick again. Except for a quick word or a wave hello as she ran errands to the buttery or springhouse, Kathleen hadn't really had a chance to talk to him since the day she was hired.

Now he escorted her down a marble-chip path bordered by peony bushes. The tightly furled blooms, promising pink blossoms as big as saucers, looked ready to burst open any moment. Kathleen felt a curious kinship with the peonies; her own emotions, locked away as tight as buds, suddenly wanted to spring free. Just a May fancy, she told herself, and pushed away thoughts of David Thornley.

They passed a formal garden of yew hedges that boxed in stone benches and marble-chip walkways edged in daffodils and forget-me-knots. Low-hanging branches of cut-leaf maples swayed gently in the soft breeze. A granite sundial stood in the center of a white clover border. Upon closer inspection, Kathleen saw that the brass plate was set upon

She shook her head, dismissing the picture. Such a life was beyond her comprehension, even if she lived to be a hundred.

Overhead, swallows swooped and arced against the twilight sky, which was tinted a pale pink. Tilting her head back to watch the antics of the birds, Kathleen imagined, for a brief moment, that she was back home, rambling over the moors with Rory.

"Is it going well with you, lass?" Patrick asked when they paused under the arching boughs of a willow.

"I guess so," she replied. "The work is hard —"

"Now, nobody ever died from hard work!" he pretended to scold. Then his gray-green eyes narrowed as he became serious. "Something's bothering you, Kathleen. What is it? Don't you like your new position?"

"It's not the job. I'm lucky to be out of the kitchen." Sighing, she confessed, "It's Tessie and Emma. Especially Tessie."

"That old broom giving you a rough time?"

She nodded, quick tears springing to her eyes. "Both girls have always disliked me from the start. But Tessie really hates me now that I have the job she wanted. One morning I found my cap and apron in the washbowl, soaking wet. I had to borrow one of Cook's aprons. The other day, my dress had been mysteriously torn, and I was late reporting for work because I had to mend it."

She didn't tell him the half of it. Aside from the malicious pranks, all instigated by

an overhanging branch and began stripping the new leaves. "It's a real pleasure to work with the Thornley horses — as fine as any I saw in Ireland. And I've managed to put away a bit of money. I figure by fall I'll have enough to send for my brother Denny."

"That's nice," Kathleen said. "I'm glad you're happy. But don't you ever get homesick?"

"Sometimes. When the day's work is done and I'm biding my time in the room over the stables, I think about home. 'Tis only natural, I suppose." His voice dropped. "I also think about you, lass. I miss you."

"I'm only next door," Kathleen said lightly, deliberately misunderstanding him.

"You know what I mean. I care about you, Kathleen."

"I like you, too, Patrick. You've done so much for me. But don't you think you ought to get out and see other girls?"

"Why should I when the only girl for me is right here?" He moved closer, and Kathleen retreated a step.

She bent to pick a bouquet of Canterbury bells that were growing in rich profusion along with sweet william and tall stalks of white hollyhock. She cherished Patrick as a friend, but he obviously felt more strongly about her. Knowing she couldn't reciprocate his feelings, she asked instead, "Do you still think America is the land of milk and honey?"

He laughed. "Well, the streets aren't paved in gold, that's for sure. But, you know, Kath-

wore a doll bonnet on his head, ears twitching with annoyance. "Oliver and I have missed you!"

Kathleen sighed. She had just dusted the drawing room and didn't relish the task of wiping ginger-colored cat hairs off the furniture. But the animal looked so ridiculous in the frilled bonnet, his ears mashed flat, she had to laugh.

"He looks like an aunt I had," Kathleen said. She was kneeling on the Oriental carpet just inside the doorway, polishing the brass doorknob. Brooks had showed her how to fit a piece of stiff parchment paper over the lock, so her oily rag wouldn't stain the woodwork.

"Aren't you supposed to be having lessons now?" she asked Pippa, who had dumped Oliver Twist on the maroon velvet settee. "Miss Devon must be looking for you," she added hopefully.

"She's taking a nap," Pippa said glumly. "She doesn't care what I do, anyway." She plopped down beside her cat as he began to wash his hind leg, evidently resigned to wearing the hat.

"How can you say that? Miss Devon is a very good governess, Cook tells me." Kathleen watched the cat out of the corner of her eye. Darned if he hadn't managed to shed on the settee already — a nest of orange hair wisped over the cushion. More work!

Pippa played with the fringed edge of a crocheted scarf that shrouded a cherry side-

opaque like Victoria's, but a clear, light brown, reflecting a sensitive nature.

"What kind of poems does he write?" Kathleen asked casually, not wanting Pippa to get the impression that she was *too* interested.

"Beautiful ones," Pippa replied dreamily. "About flowers in the springtime. And the geese that fly south every fall. He even wrote one about Oliver. I still have it. But Papa made him stop writing poems. 'Frivolous nonsense,' he called it. So David doesn't write them anymore. Isn't that sad?"

"Yes, it is. In my country, poets are held in the highest regard, next to kings. Without poets, there would be no Irish history, no one to pass on the old tales down to the next generations."

"Really? I'll tell David that. Maybe he'll want to move to Ireland." Bored with sitting still so long, Pippa jumped off the settee and bounced over to where Kathleen was dusting bric-a-brac on the ornately carved mantelpiece. "Can I help? I'm a real good duster."

"I'm sure you are, but if Brooks catches you doing my work, I'll be in big trouble." Kathleen lifted the glass shade of an oil lamp. The globe was cranberry glass with clear bands etched in intricate patterns. Brooks had told Kathleen the names of many of the art objects. Now when she carefully dusted the figurines on the wall brackets, she knew they were Meissen, imported from Germany. She knew the knotted pile rug in the dining

"Pippa! Where on earth do you get these ideas —."

A cough came from the doorway. Kathleen stopped, dustrag poised over a Haviland plate.

Tessie leaned against the doorjamb, hands on hips, her face pinched with an emotion Kathleen couldn't identify. *Did she hear what Pippa said?* she wondered.

"Cook wants to see you," Tessie said.

As Kathleen squeezed through the doorway, Tessie managed to brush sharply against her. She walked down the hall with Kathleen.

"Pumping the little girl now? I'll bet Mrs. Thornley would be very interested to know that Master David 'likes you a lot,' to quote Philippa. I wonder how long you'd last as downstairs maid if she knew. Or last in this house, for that matter."

Kathleen didn't want to hear another syllable. If Tessie was going to tattle on her to Mrs. Thornley, there was no point listening to that jeering voice another second. She ran the rest of the way to the kitchen.

Cook looked up from the chicken she was dressing. "There you are, Kathleen. I'm running behind today, and I need you to go to the market."

"But I've never gone to the market. I don't even know where it is," Kathleen protested.

"I'll tell you. Here's the basket. I need a bunch of parsnips and a bucket of butter

Chapter Nine

KATHLEEN halted in the middle of the brick walk. She wanted to turn her back and keep going, as though she had not heard. But David knew she had seen him, so she couldn't very well ignore him.

He caught up to her in a few long-legged strides. "Going to the market?" He indicated the basket she carried over her arm.

"Yes, and Cook's in a hurry, so I don't have time to chat —"

"It's such a nice day. Do you mind if I walk with you?"

What could she say? *No, I don't want you around, you make me nervous?* After all, he was her employer's son. If he wanted to walk with her to the market, she was in no position to argue.

As if sensing her dilemma, David smiled, deepening the dimple at the corner of his

hadn't called her "greenhorn" for nothing. But then, why should David Thornley be informed of a mere servant's background? Hired help came and went in the big house, and as long as things ran smoothly, who cared about the private life of a scullery girl or parlor maid? More and more, Kathleen was viewing the world through David's eyes, visualizing the vast difference between them.

He glanced at her, still waiting for an answer.

"I've only been here since mid-April," she replied. "After I got here, I worked on the —" She broke off, aware that she had nearly given away the secret of her pickpocket days on the docks. Stammering, she recovered. "I — had another job before I came to work for your father."

He didn't seem to notice her slip. "I'm surprised you've been here such a short time. You speak English so well . . . like a native."

"My mother was half English. She taught all her children to speak English and to read and write. A little knowledge, she used to say, will open doors for anyone."

"She's absolutely right. Where is she now? And the rest of your family? Still in Ireland? I've never heard you say."

Memories of those endless horrible days on the *Griffin* came rushing back. In her mind's eye she saw a sheeted body being hurled over the rail. Blinking back tears, she said, "No. My mother and father both died on the journey over here. And my brother

telling stories —" She stopped once again, embarrassed she had revealed such intimate details of her family life. Her father cutting turf . . . and sitting on a stool by the fire! What would David think?

"Your father told stories?" he asked, genuinely interested.

"All the time."

"Made-up stories?"

"Some. Mostly he told stories that his father told him, passed down by *his* father, and so on. Tales that went back to the very roots of time, Da used to say. He believed it was his duty to hand those stories down to his children, so they wouldn't be lost."

"He sounded like a wonderful man," David said, and Kathleen wondered if she detected a wistful note in his tone. "I can just imagine *my* father telling stories." He threw back his head and gave a harsh bark of a laugh.

"What is it?" she asked.

"Oh, nothing. I just had a funny picture of my father stopping in front of his bank on State Street to watch a crow fly over. The only way he'd be interested in birds was if they started carrying the latest grain prices in their beaks!"

Kathleen considered these remarks. This was the second indication she had that David didn't get along with his father; earlier that day, Pippa mentioned that Mr. Thornley forbade David to write poetry. What kind of a family was this? They had everything money

bered wind-torn clouds boiling above the mysterious gray stones and Rory lifting his arms as if calling to the Old Kings. Night-black hair and clear blue eyes flashed into her mind. And that kiss, touched by magic. Her knees weakened at the memory. Rory Limerick — her Rory — gone forever.

But David was rattling on about Boston history, unaware of her thoughts. When he related Paul Revere's thrilling ride from Boston to Lexington to warn the world that the British were coming, goose bumps rose on her arms. The words *One if by land, two if by sea* rang in her ears. David really had a gift for storytelling — as good as her father, maybe better.

"If you'd like," David said, "I could show you Christ Church where Robert Newman hung the two lanterns in the steeple. After we do the marketing, that is."

After we do the marketing. How easily two people became "we." David made the transition sound natural, as though they were destined to be a couple.

"I don't know if we'll have time," she said, unwilling to sound too eager. "Cook wants these things pretty fast."

"Oh, we'll have time. Look, we're here already," he announced as they turned onto Blackstone Street.

The market didn't have to be heralded. Kathleen could hear the peddlers hawking their wares long before the wooden stalls and

gained poorly and probably paid too much for these things. You saved me from Cook's wrath."

"Turnabout's fair play," he said. "Now you can save *me*."

"Me? How?"

"By sharing a bite to eat with me. I didn't have nearly enough dinner today, and all this fresh air has whet my appetite."

"But —" Kathleen knew she should be getting back.

"No buts." He raised a hand, as if pushing away her protests. "What do you fancy, Kathleen? Chestnuts?"

Hot, roasted chestnuts. His suggestion brought back that first rainy afternoon in Boston when she had walked down the gangplank and wandered the wharves, lost, frightened, hungry. A pushcart man had tried to sell her a pocketful of chestnuts, she remembered, but she had refused, unable to buy even one chestnut.

Now David handed a coin to a wizened pushcart man, then held his jacket pocket open. The vendor emptied his wooden scoop into David's pocket.

"Have one." David gave her a roasted nut, the hull split into flowerlike petals, revealing a nugget of nutmeat. "Eat it quick while it's still hot. Delicious, huh?"

It *was* delicious. Kathleen couldn't recall ever tasting anything so good. Was it because she was out of that house and in the spring afternoon? Or was it because she was

"That's Faneuil Hall," he said, pointing to a three-story building of rich red brick, a tall white cupola rising majestically from the roof. "We call it the Cradle of Liberty. It's a meetinghouse. Patriots gave speeches there — wonderful talks that stirred the colonists' blood, making them want, then demand, freedom."

Kathleen herself felt stirred by David's description. Freedom. Liberty. Odd words to her Irish ears. And yet they shouldn't be. Why didn't her father and the other men in their tiny village ever talk about winning their freedom from the English? The Irish were worse off than the old Colonists must have been, as far as she could see. No one was starving in the streets here. Both countries hated the British, yet the Americans had done something about it and now they were free. For a moment Kathleen wished her people had built a meetinghouse like Faneuil Hall and gave brave speeches, instead of sitting by a winter's fire, spinning old-men's tales.

How can you dare think that? she chided herself. *Da would be so ashamed. Ireland is your home, no matter what.* And America, for all its glorious past, still hated her people.

David offered her the last chestnut, but Kathleen shook her head. Her eye fell on a tiny bird of an old woman, carrying a basket heaped with ribbon-tied bunches of purple flowers.

The old woman reminded her vaguely of

later, she still contemplated Granny's words. Part of her — perhaps her English ancestry — told her that times must change. And yet she often experienced a nagging notion that she shouldn't be so quick to dismiss old ways. They were her heritage, as much as her red hair and green eyes. "Never forget the magic," were her father's last words.

"Would you like a bunch of violets?" David said, breaking into her thoughts. "Of course, you would. What a silly question." He bounded across the street before Kathleen could stop him.

"No — wait!"

But he was back within the blink of a cat's eye, presenting her with a fragrant bouquet.

She took them hesitantly. "You shouldn't spend your money on me."

"Don't be ridiculous. All pretty girls must have a nosegay of violets in May. It's practially a *requirement*." He studied the effect of the purple flowers against her burnished hair. "Believe me, the coin was well spent."

"Thank you." Kathleen buried her face in the spray of flowers to keep him from seeing her blush again. David Thornley was amazing — so different from her idea of a rich boy.

"We're going home a different way," he said. "There's something I want to show you."

"I really have to get back."

"This won't take long," he promised. "And it's right by the house, so it's not really out of the way at all."

As they hurried through residential streets,

that hemmed the Thornley estate. She thought they would leave the park and go straight home. A pang of regret jabbed her. She didn't really want this afternoon to end so soon.

But David stopped at a smooth stone. "The Wishing Stone. Part of the boulders that were blasted to make the curb around Frog Pond."

"Wishing Stone?"

"Yes. An old local legend says that if you walk around it backward nine times and make a wish, your wish will come true."

Kathleen nearly dropped the market basket. "Wish on the new moon, Kathleen," Rory's voice echoed through her mind. "Turn three times and kiss the person nearest you. If you don't look at the moon till it's new again, your wish will come true."

And then there was the crescent moon she and Patrick had seen on the deck of the *Griffin*. What had she wished for? Love. She had wished to find love.

David was looking at her, his eyes searching hers, silently telling her things she did not want to hear, things she was unable to face. Rory's face loomed between them — a wavery image, but enough to make Kathleen fall back a pace.

"I haven't wished on this stone for years," David said, his voice low. "But if running backward around this rock would give me what I want, I'd do it gladly. Do I have to resort to childhood superstition, Kathleen?"

*Chapter
Ten*

KATHLEEN hid the nosegay of violets under her pillow. The purple blooms wilted, then turned brown, but they were still beautiful to Kathleen. At night, the faint fragrance wafted upward, bringing with it treasured memories of that special afternoon with David.

But the flowers also reminded Kathleen of her dilemma. When David suddenly became serious at the Wishing Stone, Kathleen had been struck speechless. Even after she thought it over, what could she have said to him? That she was attracted to him, too? What would be gained by such an admission? He was a wealthy gentlemen, heir to a fortune, his family staunch Bostonians. She was penniless — and Irish. Nothing they could say or do would ever change those irreversible facts. Whatever David wanted from her,

at the Wishing Stone. What would Tessie do? Kathleen decided the safest course was to say nothing — neither admit nor deny her actions.

Tessie continued in the same casual voice, "The Common is pretty this time of year, isn't it? Oh, that's right, you've only been here a little while. Well, take my word for it, May is Boston's prettiest month. And Master David is *so* handsome — the perfect escort. Tell me, Kathleen," Tessie lowered her voice conspiratorially, "what did he say to make you run off like that?"

Kathleen had been baited enough. "None of your business." She pushed by Tessie to go upstairs.

The other girl moved to block her path. "Maybe not, but it *is* Mrs. Thornley's business. Anything — and anyone — that concerns her son she *makes* her business. You can believe that."

"You threatened to tell her earlier," Kathleen countered, sounding braver than she felt. "Why haven't you? Or are you just empty air?"

Tessie brought her face close to Kathleen's. "You'll see how empty I am, new girl. Just wait. The time isn't right yet, but when it is, you'd better be ready to pack your bag."

For the next several days, Kathleen walked on eggshells, half-expecting Mrs. Thornley to come into the room Kathleen was cleaning at the time and fire her. When nothing happened the first week, Kathleen relaxed a lit-

same birth month is all we'll ever have in common.

"Do you like balls, Kathleen?" Pippa tugged at the sash of the apron she wore over her cherry-sprigged dress. Her hair, probably tidy that morning, now straggled from a huge red bow.

"I don't know. I've never been to one."

"Really? Neither have I. Mama says I'm too young. If I'm good, I can watch from the stairs."

"That'll be nice," Kathleen said absently. She had reached the cherry sidetable, where a number of small knickknacks were arranged. The silver crescent-moon snuffbox stood out among the collection.

Kathleen picked it up, running her fingers over the face etched in the chased-silver lid, as she did every time she cleaned this room. There was something compelling about the snuffbox, something that drew her to it. Her hands ached with a strange kind of longing. What *was* it about this little silver box?

"I helped Patrick yesterday," Pippa said. She had abandoned her sash and was twirling an icicle-shaped perfume flagon, making the crystal bottle spin.

"Please, don't do that, Pippa. You might break it and I —" *I'd have to pay for it,* she almost said. "I'd hate to see such a pretty thing broken, wouldn't you?"

Pippa stopped. Kathleen had realized long ago that Pippa needed very little discipline and always obeyed immediately. *She can't*

"No. I never did." Kathleen's voice was suddenly distant as she recalled that evening many years ago with Granny O'Connor. Now that she thought about it, she wondered if Granny's "sight" had showed her that the O'Connor family would one day leave Ireland. Now Kathleen knew the old woman had not been talking about fairies and leprechauns when she lamented over forgotten ways. No, it was deeper than that. It was as if Granny had predicted the end of life as they knew it and that Ireland would never be the same again.

"Miss Devon says I spend too much time dreaming about fairies," Pippa said. "She thinks make-believe is a waste of time."

"Well, she's probably right," Kathleen conceded. "You *should* think about other things. Don't you have any friends your age you can play with?"

Pippa shook her head. "I like make-believe," she said stoutly. "The stories you and Patrick tell are a whole lot better than dumb old lessons."

Before Kathleen could comment on this, Mrs. Thornley and a tall, hatchet-faced woman in a stiff, black dress came sailing into the room.

"There you are!" the tall woman cried triumphantly, swooping over to the divan like a huge crow.

Pippa sat up. "Miss Devon!"

"Thought you could hide from your Latin lesson? Well, for running off, you'll have to

from Miss Devon, or you and the stable boy will be looking for new positions. Is that clear?" Mrs. Thornley's voice was as brittle as glass.

"Yes, ma'am." Kathleen dropped her eyes to the rug. Poor Pippa — to have to spend the whole day with that hateful woman. Her hand trembled as she resumed dusting, realizing how close she had come to losing her job . . . and Patrick's.

"That foolish Emma Parsley has turned her ankle," Mrs. Thornley announced to Kathleen the next afternoon. "Victoria has an appointment with Madame Foutier in half an hour. Change your dress, Kathleen. You'll accompany us in Emma's place."

Kathleen put down the small table she was carrying. Earlier that day, Brooks had announced that the downstairs rugs would be removed and the summer matting laid down. He ordered her to move all the "breakables" and as much of the light furniture as she could move out of the way as possible, so the heavy carpets could be rolled up.

"Hurry up, Kathleen," Mrs. Thornley said. "I've already called for the carriage. I don't like to be kept waiting."

"Yes, ma'am."

Kathleen raced upstairs and changed the old brown wool dress she wore on messy cleaning days, slipping the blue serge over her head.

Emma lay on her bed across the room, her

face-to-face with Victoria who acknowledged her presence with the slightest of nods. Today, Victoria was resplendent in a yellow Indian silk afternoon gown, the skirt strewn with grass-green flowers.

The costume was lovely, but Kathleen felt that yellow was unsuitable for Victoria's complexion. It made her look a little sallow, Kathleen observed, as though she had just gotten over a bad cold.

She sat quietly in the backseat, watching the sights go by and wondering what was expected of her on this outing. She wished she had asked Emma what her duties were.

"You'll have to make up your mind today," Mrs. Thornley told her daughter. "The ball is only a little over a month away. Madame Foutier is getting a bit testy. As it is, she'll have to hire extra seamstresses. And every girl in Boston is going to want a new gown for your ball."

"I don't care a scrap about them," Victoria pouted. "*My* gown has to be the prettiest. We give Madame Foutier enough business — she can afford to hire help if she needs to."

"Well, she *is* the best dressmaker outside of Paris," Mrs. Thornley added, as though she personally had discovered Madame Foutier's talents.

Victoria looked over at Kathleen, as if noticing her for the first time. "Where is Emma? I don't want the scullery girl holding my packages."

"I told you Emma sprained her ankle. And

brocade draperies. A fall of Austrian lace curtained the rest of the window.

Mrs. Thornley marched up the granite steps and pushed the bell. A small brass plate next to the bell read simply, "Madame Isabelle Foutier."

The bell was answered by a young woman who took Mrs. Thornley's and Victoria's wraps. Their footsteps were muffled by thick Persian carpets as she led them into a room with delicate gold chairs and a table on which lay several large books.

"Would you care for tea, ladies? Or perhaps something cooler?"

Mrs. Thornley plucked off her gloves, finger by finger. "Lemonade would be very refreshing, thank you."

Victoria sat down and began leafing through one of the books. She stopped at a page, stabbing her finger at the drawing. "There, that's the gown I want."

From where Kathleen stood, she could see a steel engraving of a woman wearing an elaborate gown.

Mrs. Thornley leaned over to look at the picture, reading the description at the bottom of the page aloud. "Clouded moire satin . . . Brussels lace and crystal bead trimming . . . *bronze* kid slippers. No, Victoria. You may not have that gown. It's far too old for a girl your age. Just look at that neckline — it's positively indecent!"

"But, Mama, that's the dress I want." Victoria's bottom lip pushed out as she began

crystal and jet beads, Kathleen gazed at a display of silver and pewter buckles and tried to ignore the fact that her arms were killing her. The lines of a buckle engraved with hearts and flowers intrigued her. Such a beautiful thing, she longed to examine it closer.

They left the dressmaker's and went into a nearby ladies' bootery where Victoria ordered the bronze kid slippers, a pair of pink satin dancing slippers, and a pair of butter-soft, caramel leather boots.

Surrounded by samples of dainty shoes, Kathleen was aware more than ever of her clumsy wooden clogs. When she had saved enough money, she vowed, she would come back here and order a pair of boots like Tessie's.

Mrs. Thornley stopped at a confectionary shop and bought five boxes of chocolate bon-bons. As she walked behind Victoria and her mother, balancing the odd-shaped bundles, Kathleen realized that the rich did everything differently. Even out on the streets, Victoria and Mrs. Thornley moved as though encased in a glass bubble. Nothing disturbed them, men moved aside to bow, and they had Kathleen to carry their packages.

Settled in the carriage at last, Kathleen sat back, content to listen to Victoria rattle on about her upcoming ball. She was tired; it had been a long day.

"That shade of satin is just perfect for me. Don't you think so, Mother? And those

Chapter Eleven

Cook had been so impressed by Kathleen's vegetable purchases at the market, she wanted Kathleen to do all the "in-between" marketing.

"I'll still do the big weekly shopping," Cook said, handing Kathleen a little string purse, heavy with coins. "Since I know the best meat men. But you have a real eye for vegetables and fruit. Those sugar peas you picked out the other week were so crisp, the missus still raves about 'em."

After receiving Cook's list, Kathleen took the market basket from its peg in the scullery.

The last couple of days had been drizzly and dreary, but this morning the sky looked rain-scrubbed, Kathleen observed as she let herself out the back door. The roses were in bloom, luscious, teacup-sized blossoms in pep-

"Followed me? But how . . . ?"

"Pippa saw you leaving with the market basket and she told me."

"Why would your sister tell you my whereabouts?" Kathleen wanted to know.

"Because I bribed her. Now don't looked so appalled. It's not as bad as all that. I promised to build a cat castle for that wretched animal of hers; apparently the cat has delusions of grandeur. Anyway, in return for a cat castle for King Oliver, Pippa has been watching the nursery windows, waiting for you to be sent on an errand downtown, alone." He grinned again, this time helplessly. "She had orders to let me know the next time she saw you with the market basket. And here I am!"

Kathleen was too stunned to speak. The lengths he'd taken to see her again! She didn't know whether to feel flattered or upset to be tracked this way.

"Are you through shopping?" he asked, looking into her basket.

"No. I still have to buy limes and lemons. Cook is making ices tomorrow night." She busied herself picking through the fruit so she wouldn't have to look at David. He pitched in, helping her select half a dozen of each.

"Now you're finished?" he asked hopefully.

"Yes, but I really must get —"

"No, you don't. I happen to know Cook likes you a lot, and she won't say anything if you stay out an extra hour." He took her

not really that dense, Kathleen. You don't have to beat me over the head — it's quite obvious you don't like me, although that day on the Common, I could have sworn . . ." He let the sentence die, glaring over her shoulder at the white steeple of Faneuil Hall.

If she let things end right there, her troubles with David Thornley would be over. She could stop reliving that May afternoon by the Wishing Stone. And she could forget what Mrs. Thornley had said in the carriage the other day, about David marrying Charlotte Huntley. Whenever Kathleen remembered that conversation, whether she was waxing the parquet floor in the entrance or polishing the teakwood desk in Edgar Thornley's study, she felt a sharp stitch in her side, as though she'd been running uphill.

But she couldn't let David leave this way, thinking she hated him. Because it wasn't true.

Laying her hand on his arm, she looked up into his eyes. "You're wrong," she told him, emotion bringing out her Irish accent. "I *do* like you, David, but — I'm afraid I'll lose my job if someone sees us together. Your mother has already forbidden me to talk to Pippa. I can imagine how she'd feel if she knew I was out with her son, especially since you're —" She stopped before the word *engaged* slipped out. Whatever David's future plans were, it was none of her business.

"My mother." David groaned. "I should have known it was something like that. Em-

"We'll buy things from the market," he decided. "Come on. My stomach is sticking to my backbone."

From a muffin man, David bought plump, raisin-studded muffins, still hot from the oven. An Italian sausage and a thick wedge of pungent cheese rounded out their picnic. For dessert, he splurged on ripe, juicy strawberries.

They found a bench overlooking the harbor and sat down to share the food. Within minutes, David had Kathleen shrieking with laughter as he pretended to put two strawberries in his ears.

When she was able to speak again, she asked, "You seem awfully familiar with the peddlers. The muffin man even knew your name. Do you come here often?"

He nodded. "When the weather is nice, I come down here every chance I get. I like the market, all the bustle and activity, and the exotic food from faraway places. I can think better here — get ideas."

"Ideas? Then you still write poetry?" She covered her mouth in dismay, but it was too late.

His eyebrows vaulted in surprise. "How did you know I wrote poetry?"

"Pippa told me. But she said you don't write anymore."

"Not poetry. I write stories now." He patted his jacket pocket. "I carry a little notebook around and jot down ideas. Late at

ordered to fill the shelves so they'd look good. He's never even glanced at the titles, much less read them."

"Surely he reads to relax," Kathleen said, recalling how her father loved nothing more than a full pipe and a long tale after a hard day's work. But then, her father and Edgar Thornley had very little in common.

David shook his head. "My father is a businessman. He never relaxes, and he only reads the newspaper and dull reports about banking. When he found out I wrote poetry, he threw a fit. 'No son of mine is going to waste his time on such nonsense!' "

"So you decided to write stories instead?" Kathleen guessed.

"Yes, and as it turns out, I find I like writing prose a lot better."

"What do you do with your stories?"

He sighed. "Send them to newspapers. But my stories always come back. Sometimes the editors enclose letters telling me why they can't publish my story. Once in a great while, they'll make a suggestion or two." The corners of his mouth dropped. "Father is probably right. This morning when I was working on a new story, I finally saw his point. It *is* nonsense. But, you know, Kathleen, I *hate* the idea of going to work in the bank."

"And you shouldn't work there," she declared ardently. "God-given talents shouldn't be wasted, my father always said." Hating to see him look so defeated, she asked, "Tell me about your new story. Would you mind?"

versation openers in her head when he took her arm.

"There's someone I want you to meet," he said at the corner of Revere Street. "It won't take a second. He loves company."

He escorted her across the street to a shop nestled between a tearoom and a tobacconist. JACK THORNLEY — GOLDSMITH read the discreet wooden sign over the bay window.

Without ringing the bell, David opened the door. "My great-uncle," he explained. "He's owned this shop for forty years."

Kathleen stepped through the arched doorway into the bright showroom. A walnut counter divided the width of the narrow shop. Against the far wall were smaller glass-fronted display cases.

"Well, if it isn't my favorite nephew!" A white-haired man in his early sixties stood up from behind the counter. He wore a heavy canvas apron with a tray built into the front at waist level. Carefully, he unfastened the buckles and removed the apron, which he laid on the workbench so that the tray rested on a solid surface. Then he went through the swinging gate built into the counter to join them in the front of the shop, a smile splitting his white-whiskered face.

David grabbed his uncle's outstretched hand in both of his. "Uncle Jack! How've you been? You look great."

"Just dandy. And who is this?" Jack peered at Kathleen through thick-lensed

pointed engravers. The apron tray, she noted, was filled with snips of gold wire. There were twists of gold and silver wire, and a saucer of loose diamonds and rubies glittering in the beam of sunlight that fell across the table. Protected on a square of topaz velvet lay a half-finished necklace, a heavy gold chain from which loops of diamonds and rubies overlapped, meeting a single diamond-encircled ruby in the center.

Kathleen gasped. "Ohhh. It's beautiful."

Jack put the necklace into her hands, laughing at her astonished expression. "There — now you can say you touched Mrs. Winthrop's necklace before she did!"

"I wouldn't dream . . ." Kathleen looked into the gentlemen's eyes. "You're teasing me, aren't you? Why, you're just as bad as Master David!"

"The thanks I get!" David cried, feigning hurt feelings. "Well, Kathleen, we'd better get home before your watercress dies."

Reluctantly, Kathleen surrendered the necklace, her hands remembering the smooth, yielding texture of the gold work. She had the same peculiar feeling she got whenever she dusted the silver crescent-moon snuffbox. An urge to . . . to what?

At the door, Kathleen bade Mr. Thornley good-bye, shaking his hand firmly.

"Come back anytime, little lady," he called after them. "And bring my nephew with you!"

"I like your uncle," she told David when

dropped her old wooden clogs into the box she kept under the bed.

"Nice shoes," Emma said, coming over to Kathleen's bed. She stroked the supple leather. "They must have set you back a pretty penny."

"Yes," Kathleen confessed. "They were expensive. But those clogs were giving me blisters." She wiped an imaginary speck of dust from the pointed toe of one boot.

"Aren't you the one, Kathleen O'Connor?" Tessie said, emptying the pitcher of hot water into the washbowl.

"What do you mean?" Kathleen asked warily. She put her shoes in her lap, half-expecting Tessie to try to take them from her. Life with Tessie had not improved.

"New shoes. Next it'll be a new dress. Then two new dresses. Getting real used to high living, aren't you?"

"I don't see how buying a pair of boots suddenly makes me a spendthrift."

"It isn't that," Tessie said, washing her face. "I've seen the way you dust all those pretty dishes. The statues and plates and all. You're not just careful, you really *like* those things. I bet you'd love to own them, wouldn't you?"

Kathleen did not reply. Suddenly, the new boots felt very heavy in her lap. She remembered what Patrick had told her that evening in the garden. ". . . and by fall I'll be able to send for my brother Denny." He was saving his earnings to bring his family over. And

But what could she do? If she left, quit her job, where would she go? Mentally, Kathleen ran down the list of places she had heard of in America: New York, her ship's original destination; Haverhill, the little town Tessie was from; states with odd names, Virginia, Connecticut, Tennessee. Hazy images formed in her mind of distant cities that looked exactly like Boston. She was weary of crowded streets and blank-faced ranks of brick row houses. She longed to rest her eyes on thatch-roofed cottages nestled in cool green hills, to hear the wind singing through the glen.

If she had to leave, why run to another strange, unfriendly town? Why not follow her heart back to Ireland?

At first the possibility seemed as remote as flying to the moon. But the more she considered — let the notion bloom like a rosebud unfolding — the more Kathleen realized she wasn't chained to America. She had crossed the ocean once; she could do it again. She wouldn't have to go back to the village. Instead, she could go live in Dublin where there was sure to be work.

That was it, then. She'd start saving her wages for passage back to Ireland. A one-way ticket. It would take her away from the values the Thornleys had that would never be hers. But more important, it would take her away from David, whom she knew she could never have.

she found herself thinking about David and Tessie and Patrick — problems that would never be resolved, even if she stayed in America for the next twenty years.

On her next Thursday evening off, Kathleen decided to escape. She went outside to the stables. Watkins, the groom, was currying Moonglow, David's white Arabian. Had David been out riding that day? she wondered. Why should she care? What he did with his time was none of her concern.

"Where's Patrick?" she asked the groom.

"Out." Evidently, Watkins was a man of few words.

"When do you expect him back?" Kathleen silently cursed herself for not sending word to Patrick to wait for her.

"He said about eight-thirty."

Eight-thirty. Two hours from now. Kathleen couldn't face the stuffy attic room for another two whole hours.

"I'll be back after a while," she said to Watkins. "Tell Patrick I was here."

She left the stable yard and wandered through Beacon Hill, enjoying the balmy June evening. In the lengthening twilight, children played hide-and-seek in gardens, their high, piping voices mingling with the shrill cheeps of baby birds that had hatched the past week.

She passed a couple out strolling, hand in hand, their figures softened by falling dusk. The young man leaned over and stole a kiss from the girl.

into his apron was filled with slivers and shavings of silver wire.

"I'm just about ready to clean up, anyhow." He held the door open for her.

Now that she was there, she could hardly refuse. And besides, she felt she had come to the goldsmith's shop for a specific purpose, as though she had been drawn there, pulled by a mysterious force.

"Time reveals all," her father had been fond of saying. She would wait and see what happened.

"Come take a look at my newest project," Jack invited. "I think you'll like it."

Remembering the ruby and diamond necklace from her last visit, Kathleen eagerly followed the old man through the swinging gate into the workroom side of the shop. The bench was as untidy as before, with the usual clutter of tools and rolls of gold and silver wire. But no heavy, jeweled necklace lay on the topaz velvet. Only a ring.

Jack picked it up and handed it to her. "Betrothal ring. Third one I've made this year. Unusual, isn't it?"

Kathleen had to agree. The circlet of gold was carved into a serpent, the tiny wedge-shaped head rising from the coiled body. Emeralds accented the eyes and a minuscule red-enameled tongue forked from the open mouth.

"This is an engagement ring?" she asked, incredulous. It certainly didn't seem very romantic.

Kathleen looked down at her hands, resting on the edge of the table.

"And the way you keep staring at my workbench," Jack went on, "like you're bursting with questions. Well? Aren't you?"

She shook her head, confused. What was he driving at?

He picked up an engraver and put it into her hand. Instinctively, Kathleen shifted the tool until it fit comfortably in her palm. Jack gave a nod of satisfaction. "Just as I thought. Anybody else would hold it by the handle, like a pencil. I'll bet my suspender buttons you have the knack."

"The knack for what?"

"Making jewelry."

Kathleen drew in her breath. How could he possibly know that, just from the way she looked at his workbench?

"Well?" he prompted in that impatient manner of his. "Wouldn't you like to learn the craft? I could teach you."

Kathleen let her breath out in a rush. He was right! She *did* want to work with gold and silver. At last she understood the peculiar sensation that overcame her whenever she dusted the silver snuffbox. Even now her fingers craved to pick up one of those strange-looking tools from the workbench and make something beautiful with her own hands. She wanted to create something.

"I — I don't know what to say," she admitted. "You might be right, though I would never have dreamed in a hundred years . . ."

too many years slide by. I never apprenticed a young man to take over the shop."

"You shouldn't worry," Kathleen said smoothly. "You'll probably be making jewelry another forty years."

"You Irish do have a way with words. Even so, I should be looking to the future. That's why I'm asking you to be my apprentice. What do you say, Kathleen? Would you like to learn to make jewelry?"

If the floor had opened up and the Charles River came gushing through, Kathleen could not have been more astounded. Learn to make jewelry! Actually work with gold and silver, handle glittery gems!

"Mr. Thornley, I —" She stuttered, then started over. "David didn't tell *you* the whole story, either. About me, I mean. You see, I'm the downstairs maid at his house. I work for David's father."

"So do half the people in Boston, in some way or another. So what if you're a maid? All it means is that we won't have as much time as I had hoped for. No matter." He rubbed his hands together, anxious to begin. "You don't have to make up your mind right away. Why don't we talk awhile? Have any questions?"

At least a thousand teemed to the surface of her brain immediately. One question in particular had plagued her ever since she first visited the shop. "Why do you keep all those little scraps of metal?"

"These here?" He indicated the tray built

surface, gazing into its translucent depths.

Sensing her attraction to the stone, Jack reached under the counter and pulled out a smaller wooden tray of assorted semiprecious stones. With a pair of tweezers, he picked out several opal chips and laid them on the velvet square.

"These are too small for me to fool with," he said. "But if you'd like to make a pin or a simple ring, you're welcome to the stones."

"Really?" Kathleen could scarcely believe her good fortune. Not only was the man offering to teach her to make jewelry, but he was giving her genuine opals! "That's very kind of you, Mr. Thornley. But I don't know if I should. . . ."

"Why not?" he asked reasonably. "You'll get a chance to make something pretty. As for me, well, I'll have companionship in the evenings. It gets awful lonesome here sometimes."

Loneliness was something Kathleen understood very well. Even surrounded by the Thornley household staff, she still felt like a leaf cast adrift in a stream. There were people all around but no one she could count as a real friend. Only Patrick, but their duties kept them separated for days at a time.

She was moved by the man's openness — and his generosity.

Still she hesitated. "If you truly want to teach me —"

"Nothing would make me happier. You wouldn't have to come here all your evenings

during the summer until ten o'clock, since the days were getting longer.

"It'll have to be a quick cup. I should be getting back soon."

"Won't take a minute. Make yourself at home." He bustled about, filling a kettle, taking a canister of tea off the shelf. Soon he handed her a cup of the steaming liquid and sat across from her on another stool. "You haven't worked at my nephew's long, have you?"

Although she never talked about her life before landing in Boston, Kathleen told the man about the famine, the horrible ocean crossing, and her parents' deaths. When she had finished, the silence that followed was so painful, she had to lighten the mood.

"I didn't mean to unload everything on you," she said. "Tell me about David." Where had *that* come from? She wasn't even thinking about him! Had he invaded her subconscious now, as well as her dreams?

Jack took a thoughtful sip of tea. "He's a puzzle, that boy. When he was little, he was sunny, just like his little sister, Philippa. But after he got older, he changed. I blame it on that school Edgar sent him to."

"He was sent away to school?"

He nodded. "Place way down in Virginia. Too far away, if you want my opinion. And David was too young, only eight. So he grew up away from his family, coming home only for holidays."

Kathleen had a picture of David as a little

tobacco. "You got me there, Kathleen. One's just as risky as the other, I suppose." He aimed a sharp glance at her. "You like my great-nephew, don't you? Quite a lot, from the sound of it."

She stared into her cup, as if reading the tea leaves at the bottom. "Yes. I do like him. But . . ."

Drawing on his pipe, Jack said, "I haven't lived sixty-two years for nothing. I knew about the great hunger you left. And I know an Irish immigrant's life here is no picnic."

Kathleen toyed with a small hammer, wondering what he was leading up to.

"You seem to be a sturdy young lady, Kathleen O'Connor. I'd hate to be the girl standing between you and the young man you set your sights for."

So he knew about David's engagement to Charlotte Huntley. Did this mean that he disapproved of David's choice, or was he merely trying to make her feel better? Looking at the goldsmith, Kathleen decided that he spoke his mind as he saw fit, without any obligations to spare her feelings.

"What are you telling me?"

He blew out a cloud of cherry-scented smoke. "Nothing. Only that David doesn't know his own mind yet. At least, not enough to follow his instincts."

What did Jack know that she didn't?

Setting her cup and saucer on the workbench, Kathleen bade him good-night, promising to come back on her next evening off with

that she and David had spent the afternoon together.

"Patrick, I —"

"No, don't bother explaining. It's none of my business if you want to make a fool of yourself chasing after the master's son."

"I didn't chase after him! He followed me to the market and —" She could have bitten her tongue. Why did she have to say that? Now Patrick knew that David was interested in her. Suppose this traveled back to Mrs. Thornley?

Patrick crossed his arms over his chest, a defiant gesture. "Do you like him?"

"Patrick, please let's talk about someth —"

"Answer me, Kathleen," he pressed. "Are you in love with David Thornley?"

"I don't know how I feel," she said honestly. "It's not what you think. We've talked a couple of times, and once he took me to meet his great-uncle who owns a jewelry shop. That's it." Well, it wasn't quite it. She had omitted the serious turn of conversation at the Wishing Stone a few weeks ago. She didn't want to hurt Patrick. After all, he was her only true friend in America. And she owed him a lot.

"Then you weren't with him this evening?"

"No," she said firmly.

"Where did you go?" he asked. "I've been waiting since eight-thirty."

"When Watkins told me you were out, I went to see David's uncle, the jeweler. He's a sweet old man, Patrick. Lonely. And he's

wanted to, because she didn't know them herself.

"I have to go," she told him. "Good-night, Patrick."

The lingering light in the west slowly gave up and died, allowing purple shadows to move in.

Kathleen stumbled up the stairs to the attic room, aware that her relationship with Patrick had taken a dangerous step beyond friendship. Would they ever be able to go back to carefree days? She doubted it.

In the bedroom, Emma was already asleep, but Tessie sat on the edge of her bed, watching Kathleen come in.

"How many boys," she wanted to know, "are you going to dangle on your string before you make up your mind?"

Kathleen sighed. This was not going to be a good day. Cook was already banging around the kitchen, out of sorts because her arthritis had flared up. And since Tessie had seen Patrick kiss Kathleen in the stable yard, she was ruder than ever. Kathleen shook her head, remembering Tessie's accusation that night. Did the other girl have the ability to see through walls? Nothing escaped those pale blue eyes, it seemed. And now she and Tessie had to double up on duties, which meant working together. A headache began to throb at Kathleen's temples.

"The Thornleys are having guests for luncheon today, so take care in serving," the butler cautioned her. "I have set the table for you." Kathleen felt a surge of relief. She hadn't yet mastered the intricate place setting arrangements.

"The Winthrops again?" she asked with idle curiosity, wondering if Mrs. Winthrop would wear the beautiful ruby and diamond necklace Jack Thornley had made for her.

"No. Today the guests will be Mr. and Mrs. Harrison Huntley and their two children, Miss Charlotte and Master Harold."

Kathleen's blood froze. Not *the* Charlotte Huntley, the girl David was supposed to marry? Serve lunch to David and his fiancée? Her headache roared like waves battering a beach.

She had little time to worry, since it was nearly one o'clock. When she ran upstairs to

bowl and serve from the right."

Kathleen hefted the heavy tureen onto a silver tray. "The right? But Tessie told me —" She suddenly recalled a conversation with Tessie that first night after Kathleen had been hired as scullery maid. Tessie had been bragging how competent she was as a server: ". . . Master David wants a lot of gravy on his potatoes, but Miss Victoria only takes a dab."

Darn that Tessie! Deliberately giving her wrong instructions! Suppose she had served improperly in front of David and his fiancée, or piled too much food on Victoria's plate? The thought was too humiliating.

With eyes lowered and her red hair neatly tucked into her cap, Kathleen entered the dining room. Everyone was seated and chattering away, the snowy napkins laid across their laps. Kathleen began serving the bisque, sneaking a glance at David and the girl who sat on his left.

He wore a new frock coat of soft gray linen, the shade of pussy willows, unbuttoned to show an embroidered waistcoat. The sharp points of his cream-colored shirt collar folded over a natty red cravat. He looked wonderful.

At his elbow, a blonde girl demurely spooned her soup. Charlotte.

She suits her name, Kathleen observed, taking in the honey-blonde hair tumbling over Charlotte's shoulders in a waterfall of ringlets. Diamond-studded hairpins glittered above each ear, catching a cluster of dancing

couldn't help noticing how handsome he looked in his new jacket, and the way his hair curled over his collar. His smile lit up the whole room, putting the unfortunate Harold Huntley in the shadow.

After the horrible ordeal of the luncheon, Kathleen thought she'd be able to relax with easier duties the rest of the day. But the table had scarcely been cleared when Brooks told her to report upstairs to Miss Victoria's. *Anything but Victoria,* Kathleen thought, dragging upstairs, her feet like lead.

Madame Foutier had arrived with Victoria's gown for a fitting. Kathleen knocked hesitantly on the door, then opened it to see Victoria standing on a low stool in the middle of her room, swathed in yards of ice-blue clouded satin.

Kathleen gazed around her in awe. She had never seen such a sumptuous bedroom. A fruitwood four-poster bed was curtained with pale green hangings, the color of new maple leaves in the spring. The strawberry satin comforter was topped with a dozen leaf-green and pink pillows. There were dainty chairs decorated with painted scenes and a mirrored dressing table skirted with Brussels lace. A table was cluttered with heart-shaped pin cushions, a Doulton china toiletry set, silver-backed brushes, and lavender-scented handkerchief boxes. Victoria's kingdom.

"I want the neckline lower," the dark-haired girl was saying to her dressmaker.

toria's gown in layers of tissue.

In her chemise, Victoria pouted in front of the wardrobe, both doors flung open to reveal a rainbow of dresses.

"I don't know what to wear," she complained to her mother. "I'm tired of all my clothes."

"Don't let your father hear you say that," Mrs. Thornley warned, accepting the cup of tea from Kathleen. "He claims you spend too much on gowns as it is."

"I don't care. I'm going to weed out the ones I hate, so I won't have to look at them." She poked impatiently at a hunter-green velvet cloak.

Kathleen hung up the apple-blossom organdy dress Victoria had worn at lunch and smoothed the crumpled petticoats before putting them in the lingerie chest. She helped Victoria slip into a blue-flowered dimity, aware that Victoria never really looked at her, any more than she noticed the hat rack by the door.

I don't know why Tessie is so envious of Emma's job, she thought. *I'd rather be downstairs dusting and waxing any day.*

The dressmaker left, and Mrs. Thornley retired to her sitting room to work on her needlepoint. Kathleen straightened the clutter of perfume bottles, tangled jewelry, and hair ornaments on Victoria's dressing table, while Victoria yanked gown after gown out of the wardrobe, until she was knee-deep in a pool of velvets and satins.

The wisteria darkened her eyes to emerald, at the same time highlighted the red in her hair. The dress transformed her, she noted with astonishment. The girl in the mirror was not just thin but slender. Not small but dainty and feline. No longer a parlor maid but a proper young lady.

"Where did you get *that*?" Tessie demanded from the doorway.

Kathleen whirled, her hand at her throat. "Victoria was cleaning out her wardrobe."

"And she *gave* you that dress?" Tessie's tone implied otherwise.

"She didn't exactly give it to me personally. I mean, I just happened to be standing there when she flung it at me." Her heart sank as she realized that the green gown would give Tessie one more reason to dislike her.

"And she told you to keep it?" Kathleen nodded. Tessie gave a low whistle. "You always manage to be in the right place at the right time, don't you, new girl?"

"The luck of the Irish," was all Kathleen said.

She wore the new dress on her next Thursday evening off. Earlier that week she had found a scrap of parchment in the trash and had spent two nights painstakingly designing her brooch. Especially pleased with the design she had chosen, she was eager to show it to Jack Thornley.

The old man looked sheepish. "I asked him to come by. I — haven't seen him for a while."

"So you invited him over the night you knew I'd be here?"

"You need someone to walk you home," Jack insisted, going to the door. "You shouldn't be wandering the streets unescorted."

David came in at his uncle's urging, his brows lifting when he saw Kathleen. "Kathleen! What are you doing here?"

"Visiting me," Jack put in hastily. "But I'm ready to close up shop for the night. David, will you see that Kathleen gets home?"

"Gladly." His eyes swept over her new gown, and his smile told her that she looked beautiful. He offered her his arm, which she took reluctantly. She couldn't very well refuse this courtesy in front of his uncle.

"You look wonderful," he told her as they strolled down Revere Street. "I never realized how green your eyes were before. They're almost translucent, like a bottle sitting in a sunny window."

Kathleen gritted her teeth against a sharp remark. What gall he had, flattering her only hours after entertaining his fiancée!

"Do you visit Uncle Jack every Thursday?" he asked.

"When I can," she replied without looking at him, hating to be reminded of that dreadful luncheon earlier.

planning to make jewelry for a *living*?"

"Well, I'm not exactly in a position to pick a career. But I can dream. Did you think I wanted to be a maid forever?"

"No, of course not. But —"

"But what, David? I thought you'd be happy for me."

"How can we have any kind of relationship if you're going to take up such an unfeminine occupation?"

For a moment she was too shocked to reply. Her first thought made her temper flare. How *dare* he assume she wanted a relationship, without consulting her? And while he was engaged to another girl? But the other implication of his statement fanned her spark of anger into a full-fledged fire.

"You've got a nerve, David Thornley! Moaning to me one week how no one understands you because you want to write stories. And now you use those same arguments against me. I thought you'd encourage me to do something important with my life, something that would make me happy."

"Kathleen —"

But she wasn't finished. "You say one thing, but deep inside, you just want me to be a happy little Irish servant. You're as bad as your father!"

"That's not true," he protested.

"Isn't it?"

"I'm very fond of you, Kathleen. More than . . . I have any right to, I know. I don't

watery blue eyes blinking as Kathleen came in.

"You're in bed awfully early," Kathleen said. "It can't be eight-thirty."

Tessie plucked at the hem of her sheet restlessly. "Nothing else to do."

The room was unusually quiet without Emma. Tessie clearly missed her friend.

"Out again tonight?" she asked. "Who with this time? Patrick or David? Or maybe you saw them both, in shifts."

Kathleen turned on her. "What I do on my evenings off is my business, not yours."

"You don't have to get so huffy."

"Don't I? I know you don't like me, but since the day I was hired, you've gone out of your way to make my life miserable. All because I got the job you wanted."

"Not quite all," Tessie pointed out.

"Well, I don't care what other reasons you have for hating me. But come September I'll be gone, and you can have this stupid job."

Tessie sat up. "Where are you going?"

"Home. Back to Irelend. Where people are decent. I'm saving my money now and I can't wait. Aren't you happy? You'll finally be getting your wish."

Tessie opened her mouth to comment, but a shrill scream came from downstairs, alarming them both.

David gripped Victoria's shoulders, trying to quiet her screams.

"Be still," he commanded his sister. "She'll be all right."

The butler was offering Mrs. Thornley, who was half-collapsed in a chair, a tumbler with a little amber liquid splashed in the bottom, while Cook fanned her mistress, murmuring words of comfort. Miss Devon stood nearby, wringing her hands, her gray-streaked hair hanging down her back in uncharacteristic disarray.

Tessie came in behind her and said, half under her breath, "Why is everybody in the guest room?" Between people, Kathleen saw a sleigh bed, the head-and footboards deeply curved, and a walnut washstand topped with a fine china bowl and pitcher.

Her eyes widened when she saw Patrick standing stiffly by the window, twisting his cap in his hands. Since when did Brooks relax the strict rule about stable boys being allowed in the house? Even more astonishing was Edgar Thornley, still wearing his frock coat, crouched on his hands and knees in front of the white marble fireplace, a gold watch dangling from the thick chain.

"Patrick!" Kathleen crossed the room to him. "What's happened?"

"I didn't know," he said miserably. "I didn't know she'd do it, or I never would have told her that stupid story." Under his coppery freckles, his face was bloodless.

his head toward the window, where Patrick gazed out with sightless eyes.

"I did but I couldn't get anything but gibberish from him. Some nonsense about a story." Kathleen gripped David's arm. "David, if Pippa is in danger, tell me fast. I have to know before I can help. *If* I can help."

Mr. Thornley yelled up into the yawning fireplace. "Philippa! Come down here at once!"

David passed a shaking hand over his eyes. "She was supposed to be in bed. Miss Devon was punishing her for doing her lessons poorly today and sent her to bed early. But Pippa sneaked out and went to visit the stable boy. I can't make heads or tails out of what he said to her, either, but apparently he told Pippa a story about a chimney sweep in Dublin. Then Pippa came in here — this guest room is hardly ever used — and climbed up the chimney. I guess she was acting out Patrick's story. You know what an imagination she has."

Mr. Thornley stood up then, brushing the knees of his trousers. "She's so far up there, she can't answer me," he said, his voice quivering. Kathleen wondered if he was angry or frightened. It was hard to tell with someone as stern-looking as Edgar Thornley. "What are we going to do?" he asked his son.

"Kathleen is here now," David said. "She's

brick. The rest of the child seemed to be squeezed by the chimney, like a snake about to swallow its victim.

Kathleen caught her breath. Pippa appeared to be firmly jammed into the narrow space, as far as the walls allowed. It was obvious that the child could go no farther, neither up nor down. Pippa was caught in the chimney, tight as a cork in a bottle. How would Kathleen ever get her down?

"Pippa?" she called tentatively. Can you hear me? It's me, Kathleen."

Pippa's right foot shifted slightly, loosening a cinder that fell into Kathleen's eye. She blinked it out, ignoring tears of pain.

No one can reach her, Kathleen thought. *Not even me. She'll have to get down herself.* But the little girl had to have help. And there wasn't much time to lose.

Drawing back into the guest room, Kathleen sat on the floor and pulled off her boots. Everyone in the room was watching her. If the situation hadn't been so urgent, Kathleen would have been embarrassed to be seen sprawled on the floor, her skirts and petticoats practically up to her knees, taking off her boots.

David kneeled beside her. "What are you going to do?"

"Go up after her. I can crawl up in there a little way. Not enough to reach her, but she'll be able to hear me better, at least."

In her stocking feet, Kathleen crouched on the hearth once more, tugging her skirt when

Listen to me, Pippa — if you got up here, you can get down. Just like when your cat climbs up a tree too far. What happens when Oliver gets stuck in a tree? He hollers a while and then he backs down. He's scared because he's up so high, but after he thinks it over, he sees he *can* get down on his own. Right?"

Again the foot twitched.

Kathleen blew a strand of hair out of her eyes. Nervousness and the stuffy closeness of the chimney was making her face perspire in rivers.

"Now Pippa, here is what you must do. You've got to relax your arms and shoulders. You're scared and stiff, and that's why you can't move. Pretend you're a cat like Oliver. Long and slinky. Just relax, then let yourself slide down. Ready?"

A pause, then the foot moved in reply.

"All right, Pippa. Here we go. Imagine you're a cat. You're getting slinky and limp —"

The figure above her slid down a notch. Then two inches. Kathleen backed down to give the child room. Her shoulder blades caught sharply on a poorly mortared brick, but she scarcely noticed the pain.

"You're doing fine, Pippa. Come on. A little more. Put your left foot on that brick. It's right there, just feel around for it. You got it."

At last the little girl's legs dangled above her. She could scoot down the rest of the way, but Kathleen had to get out first.

"What's the matter with you, young lady? Crawling up into the chimney like that, scaring your mother and me half to death. What are we going to do with you, Philippa?"

"I was only pretending to be Johnny Mahoney," Pippa said in a small voice.

"Who?"

"Edgar," Mrs. Thornley said, "don't thunder so. Can't you see Philippa is frightened after her ordeal?"

"Who is Johnny Mahoney?" Mr. Thornley asked his daughter in a more reasonable tone.

"He's a chimney sweep in Dublin," Pippa replied. "Patrick told me about him. He's a wonderful storyteller, you ought to hear him some time."

"Who's a wonderful storyteller, Johnny Mahoney?" Mr. Thornley ran his hand through his thick iron-gray hair. "Why is it I don't have any idea what's going on in this family?"

Pippa burst into fresh sobs and her mother glared at him.

"She's too upset to scold right now, Edgar. Let her go until tomorrow. There'll be time for sorting this out later. The important thing is, she's safe. Miss Devon, take Philippa to the nursery and give her a hot bath. I'll be in to put her to bed."

She led Pippa out of the room, with the rest of the women following.

Mr. Thornley came over to Kathleen, his hands humbly jammed into his pockets. "I

moment. "All right," he told Patrick, "you can keep your job, but from now on, mind the horses and steer clear of my daughter. The next time I won't be so lenient."

He left, waving Patrick ahead of him.

Only two people were left in the room. Kathleen smoothed the skirt of her sooty gown, self-conscious, and avoided David's direct gaze.

"Cook will clean and mend your dress," he reassured her, gingerly touching a torn sleeve. "You've hurt yourself. Your skin is scraped raw."

Kathleen was acutely aware of her bare shoulders. "It's nothing. It doesn't hurt, really. Only stings a bit."

"You ought to go straight down to Cook and let her tend to it."

His concern made her more uncomfortable than ever. She shivered.

"Are you cold?" he asked. "You must be exhausted. Here, sit down." He took off his jacket and draped it around her shoulders, then guided her to the wing chair near the window.

Kathleen sank into the chair gratefully. "I guess I am a little shaky. I was so afraid I couldn't get her out of there, David. I don't know what I'd do if anything happened to Pippa."

"You really think a lot of her, don't you?"

Kathleen considered this. She *was* fond of Pippa, more than she ever realized. Despite her resolution not to become involved with

to pluck the moon from the tarnished, brooding sky.

What was it about the moon? When was the last time she had looked up and seen it? And then she remembered . . . that frosty evening on the ship when she had wished on the new moon with Patrick, wishing that she would find love. She had failed to comply with the conditions of the charm; she wasn't supposed to look at the moon again until it was new. Had she ruined her chances?

David was suddenly very close, sharing her view out the window. "There's a halo around the moon."

He was right. Kathleen could make out a hazy ring surrounding the moon, the inner rim tinted a faint, delicate red.

She had a sudden memory of being on the marshes at dawn with Rory, two summers ago. It was the time when the moon was setting, during those white, breathless moments when everything is poised on the brink between night and day. A heron rose from the rushes, its broad-winged flight transforming the still, misty marsh, as if a signal for the world to fill with color.

There had been a ring around that moon, too, as it gradually sank beneath the frosty reeds, and Rory's face reflected those last pale seconds between dark and daylight. Kathleen had a vision that Rory would one day disappear from her life as quietly as the heron had flown across the setting moon. But

Chapter Fifteen

"**K**ATHLEEN! What a pleasant surprise. Come in." Jack Thornley held the door open wide to welcome her.

"Are you sure I'm not bothering you? After all, it is Sunday. . . ." Kathleen hesitated on the granite threshold.

Unable to spend the evening in her room, Kathleen wandered over to the goldsmith's shop, chancing that Jack would be there. It seemed rather unlikely, since everyone took Sunday off. But apparently Jack Thornley preferred to live by his own rules, even working on Sunday. Kathleen was as surprised to find him in the shop as he was to see her at his door.

"I often work Sunday evenings," he explained as they went into the workroom. "Nice and quiet around here then. Nobody ringing the bell, wanting me to fix a watch.

leen's advice on arranging a new collection of vases on the table in the morning room. Cook even fixed colcannon and soda bread for Kathleen's dinner one night. "Never hurts to try new re-seeps," she said. She always called recipes "re-seeps."

Everyone treated Kathleen with special care since Pippa's rescue. Everyone except Tessie. The blonde-haired maid still made insinuating remarks regarding the gown Victoria gave to Kathleen, even after Kathleen hung the dress on the farthest peg. Cook had cleaned and mended the dress, so it was nearly like new. Kathleen didn't give the gown back to Victoria as she intended, but she wouldn't wear it anymore, either. Sometimes she stroked the whispering taffeta, remembering the last time she'd worn it.

But even with the pleasant atmosphere in the house, Kathleen couldn't relax. On the surface, her life was a little easier, but things had not really changed. She was still a parlor maid, still thousands of miles from her homeland . . . and she still couldn't face up to her feelings for David. And there the situation would never change. It was like the simplest mathematical principle: two plus two equals four. David was wealthy; she was penniless. David came from a proper Boston family; she was an Irish nobody. No matter how she tried to switch parts of the equation around, the facts stubbornly remained the same, as if engraved in stone.

Falling in love with David Thornley, she

cleaning someone else's house, or falling in love with someone else's fiancé. With a few tools, she could create a beautiful pin or necklace. And if the pin didn't turn out right, then it wouldn't be anyone's fault but her own. Failure due to her own shortcomings she could accept.

Other forces were much more difficult to handle, though. Since the beginning of the year, she'd been buffeted about like a leaf in a hurricane, leaving Ireland against her will, watching both her parents die, living in a foreign country, picking pockets, polishing doorknobs. And falling under David Thornley's spell. She'd never have chosen to do any of those things, if she had been allowed choice. Especially loving David.

Jack left his own work to come look over her shoulder. "That's real good, Kathleen. Hard to believe you've never engraved before."

She stared at the pin critically. "Are you sure? That eye isn't too high, is it?"

"No. Even if it was, you could adjust the opal downward a little without spoiling the pin. Next week we'll set the stone, then solder the catch on the back and it'll be all finished." He patted her on the shoulder. "You've been working pretty steady. Take a break, or your neck muscles will bunch up and give you a headache. You have to learn to pace yourself."

Kathleen tried to figure out how many Thursday and Sunday evenings she'd have

on the flagstone walk outside the servant's entrance. A lighted window in the far corner of the second story drew her attention upward. She walked over to stand beneath the window, her skirt hem grazing dew-damp grass.

Since Emma Parsley left to care for her ailing mother, Kathleen had become familiar with the layout of the second floor. The yellow square of light that attracted her like a moth to a candle flame was David's window. His bedroom.

He's home, she thought, moving to hide in the shelter of a lilac bush. She saw a dark brown head bent over some task. *He must be sitting right by the window.*

After observing him for several pulse beats, she realized he was writing. *Working on the story about the girl in the fog? The one he put away?*

There was an earnestness to that bent head, framed by the soft glow of a lamp, that touched her. Kathleen's heart swelled with emotion. He was so handsome. . . . But her feelings for him were bittersweet, a heady mixture of love and yearning, tempered with regret.

It'll always be this way, she thought. *Watching him from a distance. Forever on the outside, looking in.*

He stirred just then, moving closer to the window, his hand restlessly twitching the curtain.

Kathleen shrank back against the shrub-

Kathleen said crisply, heading away from David's window. "And I was not lurking."

Patrick followed her, relentless as a bird dog. "Don't deny it, Kathleen. I saw you watching him."

"Well, so what?" she fired back. "I can look at David's window if I want."

They stopped at the garden. The stone benches crouched among the flower beds, huge and shapeless in the half-light, like mammoth turtles. Overhead, a scatter of stars shimmered against a vast backdrop of unending night sky, reminding Kathleen how very far away from home she was.

"We're not supposed to be here," she said, wondering if Tessie was watching them from a window, anxious to tell Mrs. Thornley that the parlor maid was meeting with the stable boy in the garden.

But Patrick ignored her concern. "Why don't you forget about him?" he said. "He'll never make you happy, but I can." His voice became wistful. "I'd like the chance to show you, at least. Won't you let me?" He reached for her hand and squeezed it gently.

Enveloped by the spell of the forbidden garden, night-enchanted and washed in purple shadows, Kathleen felt Patrick pull her toward him. One hand stole around her waist.

"No," she said quietly. "Please don't."

"But if you'd just give me a chance," he said again, tightening his grip around her waist only slightly.

His other hand encircled her small wrist.

Thornley's fault you didn't like me better. But now I see it's me."

"No, that's not true," she hastened to reassure him. "Patrick, you are my dearest friend in this world. You gave me hope during those dark days on the ship. Let's stay friends, Patrick. I'd hate to think that this will come between us."

"I know I'm not the best-looking lad . . ." he said, disappointed.

"Will you stop it! If you'd get out of here in the evenings, instead of mooning around the stables, you'd find out just how irresistible you are to girls. Horses don't make very good companions, do they? Go out and socialize a little. The girls will be lining up before you know it."

"You think so?" His tone sounded less miffed.

Inwardly, Kathleen breathed a sigh of relief. *It would be all right, then.* Patrick's wounded ego would heal, and they could continue their friendship. "I know so," she told him. "As a matter of fact, there's a girl who's had her eye on you for weeks."

"Who?"

She was glad to hear the old eagerness in his voice. "Tessie."

"Tessie! That old broomstick?"

"She's not really, Patrick. I know she seems a little stiff. And heaven knows she hasn't been that nice to me. But Tess has had problems at home. She's always afraid people are going to take advantage of her."

"Maybe that's all it'll be," he said. "A dream."

"What do you mean?"

"I'm afraid you're headed for heartache, Kathleen. Rich Boston boys don't fall in love with poor Irish maids. And even if they do, they certainly don't marry Irish maids."

In the nearby bushes, a single cricket began to chirp hesitantly, as if afraid to make the first call of the season.

Kathleen listened to the lonely racheting, Patrick's last words settling around her like an invisible cage. As much as she hated to admit it, she knew he was right.

the paper. As soon as the words *Wishing Stone* leaped out at her, she thrust the note into the folds of her skirt and looked around, afraid that Tessie or Brooks had seen her find the hidden paper. Fortunately, the entrance hall had been empty.

Now Kathleen trimmed the lamp wick with shaking fingers, sharply aware of the crinkling paper burning in her pocket. "Meet me . . ." he had written. Not even "Please meet me." Of course, the slip he'd written on was very small, his words cramped from edge to edge. Yet the tone of the note was more of an order than a request.

Is that so, Mr. Thornley? Kathleen's temper flared at his arrogance. *Maybe I'll go and maybe I won't.*

But as she filled the rest of the lamps, she wondered what David wanted. Since the night of Pippa's rescue from the chimney, she had only snatched the briefest glances of him. He seldom went out these days, spending hours cloistered in his room.

It was difficult keeping her mind on her work after finding the note. When she polished the heavy furniture in Mr. Thornley's study, she accidently spilled lemon oil on the floor, which had to be mopped up before it stained the straw mats. Brooks asked her three times to change the flowers in the drawing room before Kathleen retrieved the blue-and-white Delft jar and filled it with just-picked peonies, larkspur, and yellow day lilies from the garden basket.

dropped the dust cloth, imagining his farewell speech.

I can't believe he has this much power over me, she thought, clapping both hands over her eyes in a childish attempt to stop the pictures in her mind. *An unsigned note with eight little words turns my day topsy-turvy.*

She whipped around the room, flicking the dustrag over figurines and vases with renewed determination to forget him for a while. Sunlight streamed through the west windows, angling into the room, falling on the rush matting in squares of butter yellow. Kathleen fought the urge to yank the curtains closed.

When she reached the cherry table near the blue divan, she paused, polishing cloth poised over the satiny surface. Something was wrong. Cleaning this room routinely every single day had made her familiar with every object and detail, down to the last blossom in the yellow-sprigged wallpaper.

She stood back, perplexed. What was different? She counted the items displayed on the table: the pewter Jefferson cup; the mother-of-pearl inlaid picture frame with the unsmiling daguerreotype of Mr. Thornley; the ivory and jade chopsticks and fan from the Far East; the carved cinnabar snuff bottle; the enameled snuffbox shaped like a shoe. . . .

Kathleen snapped her fingers. The silver crescent-moon snuffbox! It was always next

ing three young boys flying kites farther down the green. The breeze tossed his brown hair over his forehead, and he absently whisked the forelock from his eyes.

Kathleen's heart tugged like the paper kites sailing skyward on taut strings. He looked so pensive and boyishly wistful, as if he wished he were ten again. She felt a surge of love for him. If only she could rush over and tell him ... if only he weren't the wealthy David Thornley ... if only.

If wishes were horses, then beggars would ride, she reminded herself. Brushing aside ridiculous whims, Kathleen approached the rock.

David sensed her presence, whirling away from the kite fliers.

"You came," he said simply. "I wasn't sure if you would."

How could I stay away? Aloud she said, "Lucky for you I cleaned the hall lamp first. Sometimes Mr. Brooks does it. Imagine if *he* had found your note." Kathleen kept her tone brisk, in direct contrast to her fluttery stomach.

"But he didn't," David countered gently. "And you are here."

"Yes, I am. What did you want?" *Might as well get down to cases.* Her heart threatened to stop beating altogether. Suppose he came right out and confessed he loved Charlotte? What would she do? She should be glad — that way she could leave Boston and all the painful memories of the past few months be-

been going out much lately. What have you been doing?"

He gave her a grim smile. "Writing."

"Really? That's wonderful."

"Well, I don't know how wonderful it is. I finished the story about . . . about the girl who kept disappearing. It turned out pretty good."

"What did you title it, if I may ask?" *Be still,* she ordered her racing pulse.

"Of course you can ask. You're the inspiration for the story, you know. I called it 'The Girl in the Fog.' I sent it to a paper in New York."

"Why not the Boston newspaper?"

"Because," David said, a note of pride creeping into his voice, "I have written three other stories, and I sent those to the Boston papers."

Kathleen was surprised. Four stories in a little more than a week. He really *had* been working hard. "You're very serious about your writing, aren't you?"

"It's all I want to do." His fists clenched and unclenched at his side. "There's another reason for this feverish spurt of work."

The engagement, Kathleen thought with dismay. Aloud she said, "And what's that?"

"My father. He's issued an ultimatum. If I haven't shown him that I can be a writer by July fourteenth, I go to work in his bank as a clerk the very next day. He delivered that bombshell last night after supper."

July fourteenth. That was the day of Vic-

a passing fancy. She suddenly realized why she and David could never have a good relationship, even if he weren't wealthy. He didn't treat her as an equal. It was all right for her to back his efforts to be a writer, but he didn't reciprocate.

"If only I can prove to my father that I can do it," he said, more to himself than to Kathleen.

Your life would be perfect then, she thought. *The career you want . . . and the girl.*

She gazed down the path that traversed the Common, watching two little girls about Pippa's age. Their smocks were grass-stained and their stockings sagged from an active day of play. Dandelions poked through their tangled curls, and chains of daisies hung around their necks.

Pippa should be out here, playing with children her own age. Kathleen knew the little girl spent the hours between lessons and bedtime playing with her cat or the many toys in the nursery cupboard. The wooden Noah's ark with its carved wooden animals — a proper, instructional toy endorsed by Pippa's parents — seemed a poor substitute for daisy chains in the magical June twilight.

"I'm glad you came here," David said softly, as if succumbing to the same deep-summer sorcery. "I needed to see you. You're good for me, Cat. When I start to lose sight of my goals, you set me back on track. You're a real lifesaver. And that's not all —"

at her nerve failing her when she wanted to know about Charlotte Huntley.

The laughter of the little girls and the cries of the kite fliers grew faint. *No point staying here any longer.*

Gathering her skirts in one hand, she told him, "I have to go now, David. It's late and I have to get up early tomorrow."

Before he could protest, she left him standing by the Wishing Stone as shadows cloaked the Common for the night.

"Kathleen! Come here a moment!" Victoria's imperious tone carried all the way down the hall.

Kathleen gritted her teeth as she shifted the heavy stack of linens. What did that girl want now?

With Emma gone, Kathleen and Tessie divided the upstairs chores, switching routines every other day. Kathleen hated upstairs duty; downstairs she could clean and dust without being bothered. But up here, she could scarcely get anything done without Victoria pestering her to find her lace glove or button a cuff.

She stored the freshly pressed linens in the cupboard at the end of the hall, then went into Victoria's room.

"I told you to come here, not put sheets away," the dark-haired girl said, vexed.

"I'm sorry." Kathleen obstinately refused to add the required "Miss Victoria." "I couldn't very well drop them on the floor, and

"You think because I look at your brother I'm interested in his money?"

"Aren't you?" Dark brown eyes drilled into Kathleen. "You and every other girl in Boston want to snare my brother. Now you see why I make it my business. David stands to come into a lot money one day —"

"I don't care if he's the richest man in the world! For all the money your family throws around, I haven't noticed that anyone is happy here. Your mother only smiles when she's bought something new, and Pippa would ten times rather be outside playing than locked in the nursery with that dreadful Miss Devon. And you —" She broke off, horrified. She'd never learned to curb her tongue, and this outburst would probably cost her her job.

Victoria's lips curled into a wry smile. "Do go on. This is most interesting. What were you going to say about me?"

Kathleen dropped her gaze to the floor. "Nothing," she whispered. Never in a hundred years would she tell Victoria that despite her fancy wardrobe, she was obviously a lonely girl. Beautiful as Victoria was, only pasty, stammering Harold Huntley called on her.

"Nothing," she said again. "I spoke out of turn. It won't happen again."

"No, it won't." Victoria took a step closer to Kathleen. "After I tell you this, you won't be quite so sassy. Did you know that my birthday ball will actually celebrate two

Chapter Seventeen

KATHLEEN unwrapped the scrap of velvet and studied her pin in the lamplight of Jack Thornley's workroom. At last, it was finished.

The crescent moon brooch was far from perfect: the curved sides were a little bumpy in places and the moon's face seemed somewhat off-center; but she was proud of her handiwork. The opal chip she had chosen to accent the eye glittered a soft, misty green with glints of blue and gold.

Holding the pin in the palm of her hand, a thought struck Kathleen. Since arriving in America, she had been haunted by new moons.

Jack left the ring he was working on to come stand behind Kathleen's stool. "You ought to be proud. You did a fine job on your first piece. And that design looks simple, but

"Uncle Jack, please listen. I have something to tell you. I want you to sell my pin — that is, if you think it's worth anything."

He stared at her, a garnet between two fingers, the lamplight fracturing the unusual color into tiny green rainbows. "Sell your brooch? But why?"

"I need the money," she stated bluntly. "I'm — I'm going home. Back to Ireland."

"Ireland?" His face was wrinkled with bewilderment, as though she had suddenly started speaking Gaelic.

"Yes. And I don't have enough money saved for passage. At first I thought I'd save my salary. I would have had enough to leave in mid-September. But something . . . has come up, and I want to go right away. I-I'd rather not wait any more."

Jack dropped the garnet onto the satin and absently rerolled the packet, securing it with the ribbon. "Something's come up, eh? Would that something — or someone — be my nephew David, by any chance?"

A vein jumped in her temple. She could see Jack was not going to let her leave so easily. "I don't want to talk about it, Uncle Jack. Please."

"I think you have to. You're like a granddaughter to me, Kathleen. I've become very attached to you. And I think you like me, too. Don't I deserve an explanation?"

"Of course you do!" she agreed in a rush of affection for the old man. "I guess — I thought if I could get away quickly, I wouldn't

because of that? Is that it?" The jeweler raised his bushy eyebrows in surprise.

Now it was Kathleen's turn to be surprised. "What do you mean, is that it? Isn't that reason enough? Have you ever suffered rejection, Uncle Jack?"

"More times than I care to count." He chuckled. "But we're not talking about me. We're talking about you. And David."

"Haven't you heard anything I've said? There is no David and me. It's David and Charlotte."

"Not necessarily." Jack stroked his whiskers thoughtfully. "Before we tackle that subject, there's something I have to know."

"What?"

"Are you going back to Ireland because of David, or is there another reason? Something else you haven't told me."

"Yes, there is. As you said yourself one time, life in America for the Irish is no picnic. Patrick tells me about the shanties in the North End where our people are living, not much better off than when they were starving at home. And down on the docks I know — well, I've *heard* — how people have to live. Patrick and I both thank our lucky stars we have good jobs with room and board. But outside the Thornley estate, things aren't so rosy. Everywhere I look there are those hateful signs, NO IRISH NEED APPLY. What will become of the Irish in America?" As she remembered the conditions of the homeland she had left last February, she added, "For

"Well, they're getting along fine now," Kathleen said, unable to keep the bitterness from her tone.

"Do you know that for a fact? Have you seen them together?"

"I told you about the luncheon —"

He waved his pipe impatiently, dismissing that incident. "No, I mean together, like in the parlor or out strolling. A luncheon with parents present hardly counts."

Kathleen shook her head. "I only saw her that one time."

"Then aren't you jumping to conclusions?"

"David told me they were getting married —"

Jack cut her off with a jerk of his pipe. "That's not what you said a few minutes ago. David only told you what his and Charlotte's parents intended — not what *he* intended."

Kathleen thought this over. It was true. David had never actually admitted that he was going to marry Charlotte. . . .

"You didn't give up when you were tired and hungry," Jack reminded her softly. "Or when your parents died. Don't give up now, Kathleen, if you truly care for my nephew. And I think you do. Stay till summer's end, at least. If you still want to go back to Ireland I'll buy your pin myself — I'd never sell it to a stranger — so you'll have enough money for the fare."

His offer hung in the air between them. Kathleen reached for her brooch, fingering the catch soldered to the back. She didn't

find a way to speak to you ever since — since the other day."

Kathleen wasn't ready for this. After her talk with Uncle Jack, she'd decided to meet with David to see if they could reconcile their differences, but she wanted to see him on her own terms, when she was prepared. Why did he always have to force the issue, catching her off guard?

"David, I — it's going to rain," she said stupidly. Already her resolution to confront him rationally was swirling away, dissipating into the charged atmosphere. Confusion surged in its place, like a wave rushing to fill a hole in the sand.

"Listen, Kathleen. I left a dinner party to find you. The least you can do is give me a chance." His hand brushed her loose hair away from her face. "Everything I want to say to you just flies out of my head when I see you like this. Your hair looks so silky and . . . what's this?" He noticed the brooch. "That's very pretty. Did Uncle Jack give it to you?"

Kathleen could scarcely trust her ears. "Do you really think it's pretty?"

"Of course. Is it a present from Uncle Jack?" he pressed. Kathleen suspected his sudden concern was a jealous reflex, that he probably wondered if another boy gave her the pin.

To put his mind at rest, she confessed, "Jack didn't give it to me. I made it myself."

So, he thinks he has me over a barrel, does he?

Kathleen said tartly, "I'm not staying in here with you a second more than I have to."

"I see the rain didn't dampen your temper any. Now, where were we before the heavens burst?"

She folded her arms across her chest, glaring at him. "What are you talking about?"

"Our discussion. We were arguing about that pin. You deliberately went back to Uncle Jack's shop after I told you how I felt about your learning to make jewelry."

"As I told your sister the other day, my private life is my affair. I'm getting pretty tired of you Thornleys trying to own me. I'm not your serf."

"I never said you were. You bring that up every time, Kathleen."

"Only because you people have a habit of keeping us poor people in our places. What's wrong with wanting to make my life better?"

"Not a thing. But can't you do something more feminine? Like dressmaking? Or millinery?"

"Making hats!" she spat. "I don't want to fuss with feathers and prissy women who don't know what they want. I want to be a goldsmith, like your uncle. Why don't you want to be a clerk in your father's bank?"

A tiny muscle twitched in David's jaw. "That's not fair, Kathleen. There's no comparison."

"Oh, no? I happen to think otherwise. Or

to be different. David should have been her closest ally, but instead he was rapidly becoming her biggest enemy.

"What are you thinking, little Cat?" he asked softly.

She was aware that he was standing close to her and that the rain-curtained doorway was very small . . . and private.

"Nothing," she replied haltingly. "I wasn't — thinking anything."

"I can't believe that," he murmured, his mouth brushing her hair. "Your mind always seems to be busy. Don't try to play the empty-headed flirt, Kathleen. I know better."

She tried to move around him but came up against the other wall. "Is the rain letting up?" she asked hopefully.

The corners of his eyes crinkled with amusement. "Why? Don't you want to stay here forever? I do."

His hands spanned her small waist, causing her to gasp in surprise. "You are so tiny," he said. "My hands practically meet."

His hands were warm bands, gripping her waist confidently. Surely, he would kiss her. She couldn't imagine which would be worse — if he kissed her or if he didn't. She wanted to relax in his embrace, lean against his chest and put their differences aside for a few moments.

"David . . ." she resisted weakly.

"Cat." His voice dropped to a whisper. "Don't disappear, please. Don't leave me like the girl in the fog."

"I want you to — you should know I'm taking Charlotte Huntley to Victoria's party."

Kathleen thrust him away from her.

"Don't look at me that way. I wouldn't go with her, but our parents insist we attend together —"

"You've got nerve, David Thornley!"

"Cat —"

"Don't Cat me! No wonder your father pushes you around! If you don't ever stand up to him, you'll never be a writer. And if you don't make up your mind which girl you want to court, you're going to be sitting alone one of these days. Have a good time at the ball," she concluded huffily.

Before hurling herself into the drenching rain, she launched a parting shot. "And another thing. I intend to keep making jewelry, whether you like it or not!"

wisp of wind stirred the wisteria trees in the garden. Yet there was an air of anticipation about the stillness, as though something important were about to happen.

"At least you're in the house," Patrick said enviously. "Swap you the stables for the drawing room any day."

Kathleen giggled as a picture rose in her mind — Patrick, swathed in a starched apron, dusting the delicate porcelains in the drawing room.

"Patrick, don't be so foolish. Listen, I've been thinking —"

"Whoa, now!" He threw his arms up, fending off an imaginary attack.

"Stop it," she scolded, unable to stop laughing. "Be serious."

He straightened up, an incongruous frown marring his boyish features. He cleared his throat dramatically. "Would you be mistaking me for a professor?"

"Hardly." Kathleen managed to curb her giggles at last. "I want to ask you something. I've been thinking about us —"

His eyebrows quirked upward. "Us? You mean you and me?"

"Not just you and me — but all the Irish in this city. What do you think it would take to change the way Americans feel about us?"

He scratched his chin, considering. "Well, fisrt of all, I guess it'll take time. People here need to get used to us, and we need to get used to them. Mostly, I think we have to prove ourselves — you know, show them we're not

famous goldsmith. Won't that combination make Boston sit up and take notice?"

"Sure, and it would be grand. So you still have your heart set on making jewelry?"

"If I stay —" She stopped too late.

"What?"

"I mean, if I can," she amended hastily. "If Uncle Jack wants to go on teaching me." She hadn't told Patrick her plan to return to Ireland. Surprisingly, no one on the Thornley estate knew, even after Kathleen blurted her secret to Tessie. For some mysterious reason, the other maid had never said a word. And for now, that was the way Kathleen wanted it.

"I've got to run," she said, wiping her sticky hands on her apron. "Brooks has us all working like fiends today."

Preparations for Victoria's birthday ball had the entire household whipped into a whirl-wind of cleaning and cooking. As Kathleen walked through the kitchen, Cook was marshaling her temporary staff — extra help hired for the occasion — giving them brisk orders. Six market baskets, piled with fresh vegetables and fruits, sat on the scrubbed worktable, waiting to be unpacked.

Kathleen's excuse to get away from Patrick was not false. The butler kept both Tessie and Kathleen hopping all afternoon, polishing and waxing every inch of the first floor. From the library windows, Kathleen saw gardeners swarming the grounds, clipping hedges and pruning trees. The dressmaker and her assis-

the hope for relief later that night.

As she flipped the sheet, something small and hard clattered to the floor. "What's this?" She bent to pick up the object that had rolled under the bed. Her fingers closed over a solid, vaguely familiar shape.

"The snuffbox!" she whispered, staring incredulously at the silver crescent-moon box lying in her hand. "How on earth did it get —" Suspicion dawned into realization. "Tessie Whittaker!" she cried. "You put this in my bed! Why?"

Tessie said nothing.

In five angry strides she was at the window, holding the silver box out to the other girl accusingly. "Tell me, Tess. I want to know why you did it."

Slowly, almost insolently, Tessie set the brush on the windowsill. "If it weren't for the haze, you could see clear across the Common. A few nights ago, though, there wasn't no haze."

"I know what you're driving at," Kathleen said, on to Tessie's methods by now. "You saw me with David by the big rock, isn't that it? What does that have to do with putting the snuffbox in my bed? If Mrs. Thornley discovers it's missing, she'll —" Kathleen halted, dumbfounded by the implication of her words. To be branded a thief — whether or not it was true — was immediate grounds for dismissal.

"You're trying to get me fired! What happened, Tess? Did your little plan backfire?

behind the bland blue eyes. "It's not just the parlor maid position, is it? What else? What else about me bothers you so much that you'd go to such lengths to have me fired? It is because I can read?"

Tessie whirled on Kathleen. "I don't care about your book learning. I know how to do lots of things you can't find in books. If you must know, Miss O'Connor, I'm sick of the way everybody toadies to you."

"Toady?" Kathleen tried the term on her tongue. "What does that mean?"

"Everybody likes you. Cook thinks the sun rises and sets with you. Brooks gives you special treatment. And since you got Miss Philippa out of the chimney, you can do no wrong with the missus."

"Where do you *get* such ridiculous notions?" Kathleen asked, more aggravated than angry. Honestly, Tessie acted like an eight-year-old sometimes. "Mrs. Thornley smiles at me once in a while, and Mr. Thornley can barely remember my name. Cook is nice to everyone, and Mr. Brooks does not give me special privileges."

"What about last week when he let you arrange the flowers? He never let the parlor maids do that before," Tessie pointed out.

"I guess he knows that I like working with plants and flowers. Being Irish, I feel a kinship with growing things."

"Still, everybody likes you best," Tessie insisted petulantly.

"And why is that?" Kathleen was deter-

you came along and everybody could see straightaway you were faster and smarter than me. If I didn't watch out, you'd work me right out of my job."

"But that's not true," Kathleen argued. "The first day I came here, Cook told me what a good server you are. And you still serve most of the meals. I've only filled in a couple of times."

"Cook said that about me?" Tessie blinked with surprise. "Usually she tells me not to fuss over the trays."

Kathleen smiled. "That's just her way. You know how she is — all that gruff hides a heart of gold."

"I *can't* lose this job," Tessie said vehemently. "I just can't! I refuse to go back home."

"The farm is that terrible?"

"More than you'll ever know. I couldn't wait to get away. And I won't go back, even if I have to live on the wharf."

Kathleen shot a glance at her. Did Tessie know Kathleen's background? How could she? Kathleen kept those early weeks in Boston a secret; only Patrick knew, and he swore he'd never reveal the truth. Giving Tessie a sidelong glance, Kathleen decided she meant no harm — it was only a chance remark.

Tessie went on. "You should see my mother — nothing but bones. She works like a dog on that farm, raised eight children. And what does she have to show for it? A ramshackle

"He's . . . such a nice-looking young man. And so cheerful. Always ready with a wave or a bright hello."

"That's Patrick," Kathleen agreed. "Any girl who wins him should consider herself lucky."

Tessie faced Kathleen, her eyes round with shock. "You mean . . . but I thought Patrick liked *you.*"

"He does. As a friend. That's all. Oh, I know Patrick thought we meant more to each other for a while, but we're really just good friends. Patrick isn't very sure of himself — I think he's afraid of girls. That's why he thought he liked me. We're both Irish and we've been through so much on the ship . . . but he likes America so much, I think he wants to settle down with an American girl."

"Do you . . . do you suppose he might be interested in walking with me some evening?"

"Why don't you ask him? He's awfully shy, so you'll have to go to him. But it'll be worth the effort. Patrick is funny and kind — the best." She patted Tessie on the shoulder. "Give it a try."

"I feel so horrible about the things I said to you," Tessie said miserably. "Taking the snuffbox, trying to get you in trouble all these weeks. I hope you don't hate me too much."

"I don't hate you at all," Kathleen replied. "I never did. It's just too bad we couldn't

was ripping seams, it looked at though she might not get to bed at all.

"Pippa! What are you doing up at this hour? Miss Devon will give you a good scolding if she finds you down here."

Kathleen had gone down to the kitchen where the lighting was better. Wide awake now, she wanted to finish hemming the gown she and Tessie had altered that night.

She looked up once to see Pippa, in a lace-trimmed chemise and bare feet, slip through the door, the ever-present Oliver Twist at her heels.

"I'm not sleepy," Pippa said, coming into the kitchen. "Miss Devon made me go to bed even earlier tonight. She says I'm too excited about the ball tomorrow. Can I sit in here with you? I won't bother you, I promise."

"You're not a bother, Pippa. Sit down. I'll fix us some hot milk." She poured some milk into a small pan and set it on the stove, stirring the banked embers to life. *Poor Pippa.* Ever since the chimney incident, Miss Devon followed her charge around like a watchdog, never letting the child from her sight.

When Pippa had sipped her drink, licking at the milk mustache that glazed her upper lip, she said, "Know what I wish?"

"No. What?"

"I wish you were my sister. My real sister."

"That's awfully sweet, Pippa, but you have a sister."

Chapter Nineteen

Moonlight transformed the garden into another world. Japanese lanterns strung from tree to tree twinkled their fairy light, and moths circled the paper shades on transparent wings.

Above the full-leaved wisteria trees, a half moon tilted downward, spilling moonbeams on the gathering below. A scatter of blue-white stars glittered above the musicians and dancers. Tinkling laughter broke into the soothing notes of a Strauss waltz.

Hidden under the lilac bush, Kathleen observed Victoria's party from her leafy, sweet-scented bower, her eyes following the graceful movements of one couple in particular. David and Charlotte. They danced so beautifully together, gazing into each other's eyes as if they could waltz forever.

ruffled apron bodice, she had pinned her brooch where it could not be seen. The pin brought her a kind of comfort, her badge of future independence, and a symbol of hope that one day she would control her own destiny.

With nervous fingers, Kathleen fluffed the bow on Tessie's apron. "Are you sure I'll be all right? I haven't served since — since that luncheon a few weeks ago." When she'd first seen the lovely Charlotte Huntley.

"You'll be fine," Tessie said, adjusting the streaming ribbons of the white net caps they wore for the occasion. "I'll take the left side of the table. You take the right. That way we won't get tangled up."

As they carried in the soup course, Kathleen's initial impression was that the dining room was packed with chattering, laughing people.

"I thought this was an intimate supper," she whispered to Tessie.

"This *is* intimate," Tessie whispered back.

Every seat around the oval table was occupied. With a fluttery pulse, Kathleen ladled mock-turtle soup into bone-thin china bowls rimmed with ruby. She recognized Mr. and Mrs. Thornley at opposite ends of the table.

Victoria sat at her father's right, cool and resplendent in ice-blue clouded satin, sapphire drops dangling from her earlobes — a gift from her parents — an indulgent smile on her lips. Kathleen knew that hidden under the billowy satin skirts, Victoria wore the bronze

He held his fork easily in his right hand as he ate the squab. In that casual, unaffected gesture, Kathleen realized a universe of differences between them. The sterling fork looked so *right* in his hand. He handled the flatware piece — which, if sold, would have fed half of Kathleen's old village — as though it were his birthright to to be surrounded by gold and silver.

And so it is, she observed sadly. Whatever had she been thinking all these weeks? David Thornley, gentleman, heir to a fortune, was the perfect suitor for the airy, equally wealthy Charlotte.

If I held that fork, she mused, *it would probably tarnish.*

A discreet nod from Mrs. Thornley snapped Kathleen from her trance. As she passed the gilt-framed mirror hanging near the door, she hastened to steal a glance at her own reflection.

Against the backdrop of the dinner party, the colors muted under the sparkling chandelier, Kathleen decided she seemed unnaturally bright — the hair straying from the lace cap a blaze of reddish-gold, her eyes like emeralds held up to a sunlit window, two spots of pink high on her cheeks. Under her apron, her brooch burned like a firebrand. A message flashed through her mind: *Something is going to happen tonight.*

I don't belong here. I never will, she told herself. She served the rest of the meal without looking at David.

Give me a chewy cookie and you can keep your mouthfuls of air."

Yes, Kathleen agreed silently. *Give me a solid relationship with a boy. No castles in the air.*

When the dishes were washed and Cook comfortably settled, the girls were dismissed.

"You can watch the party," Brooks told them, "but stay out of sight."

Kathleen and Tessie took off their aprons and caps, patted their hair as if they were late-arriving guests, then slipped out the servant's entrance.

Patrick came by, and soon he and Tessie wandered away. Left alone, Kathleen found the lilac bush gave her the best vantage point for watching the dancers without being seen.

The waltz over, the guests clapped and dispersed. Kathleen waited for David to reclaim Charlotte, but she was heading for a stone bench, her gloved hand tucked under the arm of another young man.

David left the group, walking toward the lilac bush, his hands deep in his pockets. *How does he do that?* Kathleen wondered. *Manage to look like a little boy out here — and a drawing-room gentleman at supper? Which is the real David Thornley?*

His moods and expressions shifted faster than the wind.

She peered between the branches again. He was coming her way! Suddenly, she wanted to bolt, but her knees were locked, her feet frozen. She felt like a small animal about to

heart was crumbling, she couldn't hurt his feelings. "I'm sorry," was all she could think to say.

"Sorry? I'm not — do you think I'm upset over Charlotte?"

"Well, aren't you?"

He gave a short laugh. "Lord, no. It's bad enough I had to be her dinner partner. I'm only too glad to let some wide-eyed admirer take her off my hands the rest of the evening."

Kathleen was so taken aback by this reversal in attitude, she nearly fell over. "David, I don't understand. I thought —"

He reached out and took her firmly by the shoulders. "I can imagine what you've been thinking, Kathleen. I watched your face when you served supper earlier. You thought I was really enjoying Charlotte's company, didn't you?"

"But I saw —"

"You *thought* you saw. Things aren't always as they seem, Kathleen. That's what I'm trying to tell you."

"You mean, you were *pretending* to have a good time?"

His voice suddenly became weary. "With every fiber. It was all a sham — the witty remarks, the flattery, all of it forced. I tried to tell you the other night I was only with Charlotte because our parents expected it."

Kathleen's head was reeling. She'd been miserable for days over nothing? Every time she and David were together, he managed to

self. *A moon-drenched waltz at midnight?* She wished she could bottle this moment in a crystal jar but knew she could never capture this feeling any more than she could gather moonbeams in a net.

The waltz ended — Kathleen could hear the guests clapping politely — yet David continued to swoop her around their open-air ballroom. At last he slowed, as if reluctantly realizing that the dance was over, but he did not release his hold right away.

"Thank you, Cat. That was the most special dance I've ever had."

"Me, too," she murmured. Something in his tone disturbed her — a lilting sadness, as though he were really telling her farewell. She stepped back a pace, anxiously searching his face.

"David, what does this mean? I thought you said you don't really love Charlotte? Yet you seem —"

"I don't love her. I never did. You are the only girl for me, Kathleen. I love you. You must believe me."

His declaration set the stars spinning again. How she had longed to hear him say those words.

"I believe you, David. And I love you, too," she said simply and honestly, ready to give him her heart. Would he kiss her now? Her body leaned toward him.

He took her hands instead. "Kathleen, I'm afraid I've done nothing but make you miserable. I went to see Uncle Jack last night, and

"David, for heaven's sake, what *is* it?"

"Kathleen, I just want you to know —"

Suddenly, a voice rang out. "David! Where are you?" Victoria was coming their way. "David! Father is ready for you!"

Kathleen clutched his sleeve. "Your father? What does he want?"

"I can't — Kathleen, please remember I never wanted to disappoint you."

Bending swiftly, he kissed her on the lips. Kathleen's protest died in her throat as she clung to his coat, lost in the most enchanting moment of the evening. All too soon the kiss was over. He broke away, leaving her by the lilac bush.

"What are you doing out here?" she heard Victoria ask her brother.

"Never mind," David replied curtly.

"Let's hurry. Father is ready to make the announcement."

The announcement! Kathleen's legs turned to water. So that was what he had been trying to tell her — he was going to marry Charlotte after all, in spite of vowing his love for Kathleen.

Numbly, she heard Edgar Thornley's voice booming over the lawn as he began the announcement. Tripping over her skirts, Kathleen stumbled toward the servant's entrance. There was no way she would listen to those horrible words.

Welsh cupboard, and poured tea from the steeping pot. She'd never acquired a taste for coffee, which Americans seemed to drink by the gallon.

"Reckon you didn't sleep any better than I did," Cook went on, mistaking Kathleen's silence for early-morning grogginess. "That racket outside kept me awake till all hours. Then they expect us to jump up at daybreak and get busy while they lie around half the afternoon."

Kathleen knew Cook's leg was bothering her again, from the way the older woman stumped heavily from pantry to stove, limping slightly and referring to her employers as "they," as though the Thornleys were an unseen enemy.

She sipped the strong, hot tea, listening to Cook's one-sided tirade, wishing she were anywhere else in the world but this house. Staring deeply into the dark amber liquid, a hint of cinnamon rising with the steam, Kathleen tried to will away unwanted memories of the previous night, which crowded into her mind. But she couldn't.

She heard Mr. Thornley's voice echoing in her ears as that terrible scene replayed, eclipsing the bright morning sun. After David had left with Victoria, Kathleen dashed across grass slick with dew, ran upstairs to the attic bedroom, and collapsed on her cot in a spasm of sobs.

Her face crushed against the pillow, she cried for her family, gone forever, and for

you missed Ireland in all these weeks. And tonight I come up here and catch you crying your eyes out."

"I guess it just caught up with me," Kathleen said weakly.

Tessie's answering silence was laced with skepticism.

Kathleen asked hastily, "Aren't you getting in kind of late? What did you and Patrick do this evening?"

The other girl's features softened in the golden candlelight, and her voice took on a dreamlike tone. "We went strolling through the Common, just like I've always wanted. We sat on the bench near the pond and watched the moon shining in the water. Kathleen, it was *so* romantic. We talked the longest time. Patrick told me about wanting to own a horse farm in Tennessee one day. And he'll do it, too," she added with pride. "He's real determined. And smart, too! After a while, I got a little chilled, and he gave me his jacket to put over my shoulders. When he walked me home, he held my hand."

Kathleen smiled through her misery. So true love blossomed in the park! How wonderful for Tessie.

"I'm glad for you," she told Tessie. "I hope . . . I hope you and Patrick will be very happy." The last words broke as fresh sobs racked her small frame.

"Kathleen, what is it?" Tessie demanded, alarmed. "And don't give me that homesick story. Someone has hurt you. . . ." She drew

real." But Kathleen remembered the tenderness shining from his clear brown eyes, the gentle caress on her cheek. And she hadn't just imagined those wonderful afternoons at the market, the moonlit evenings in the park.

"It's not fair," Tessie said. "First you have two boys attracted to you and I didn't have anybody. Now I have Patrick, and you —"

"Don't have anyone," Kathleen finished for her.

"I'm sorry. I didn't mean —"

"It's all right. I *don't* have anyone. And I'm not sure I ever did."

"I feel so guilty," Tessie admitted. "Coming in here all excited and bubbly, while you —"

Kathleen laid a comforting hand on the other girl's arm. "I'm glad for you and Patrick, I truly am. Hang on to the happiness as long as you can." *You never know when it'll vanish.*

Despite the late hour, the rest of the night passed slowly. Between midnight and dawn seemed an eternity for Kathleen. Because their windows faced the front of the house, party noise did not reach them. Tessie fell asleep almost immediately, but Kathleen pitched restlessly on her narrow cot. When the party broke up, good nights resounded over the front lawn, and carriage wheels crunched the gravel as the guests departed.

Even after all was still, Kathleen couldn't surrender to sleep. She lay awake, counting

the other servants be gossiping about David's engagement? Cook hasn't said a word, and she usually knows everything that happens around here before anyone else."

Tessie expertly sliced a lemon into fan-shaped wedges. "You're right. Something strange is going on."

Cook stomped by. "Move, Tessie. Mr. Thornley would like his coffee before dinner-time."

"I'm moving." Tessie gathered the tray and backed through the swinging door.

Kathleen dawdled over her teacup, loath to begin the day's chores. The lamps had to be cleaned and filled. The dining room and drawing room both needed a good going-over after the supper party last evening.

Suppose she ran into David? Meetings were unavoidable even in a house of this size. What would she say to him? Could she keep the hurt from showing in her eyes? Of course, he should act embarrassed. Maybe the idea of meeting her would make him so uncom-fortable that he'd take special pains to keep out of her way. Perhaps —

"Kathleen!" Tessie bumped through the door, waving the silver tray.

From the stove, Cook gave her an odd look but said nothing.

Tessie rushed over to the table, banging the silver tray on the knife-scarred top. "Kathleen, you'll never guess what's hap-pened!"

"Tessie," Cook called over the spattering

still asleep and Pippa always ate in the nursery with her governess. Only Mr. Thornley, Mrs. Thornley, and David sat at one end of the table. And they were all quarreling.

Kathleen slipped into the room and set steaming dishes on the table; at breakfast, the Thornleys liked to serve themselves.

But today no one reached for the bowls or sent Kathleen back to the pantry for another pot of jam. She stood next to the sideboard, waiting for Mrs. Thornley to request that she pass the plates. No one noticed Kathleen or touched their cooling cups of coffee.

"Don't be too hard on your father," Lydia Thornley was telling David. "He's only doing what he feels is best for you, aren't you, dear?"

David rubbed his forehead wearily. "What's best for me," he echoed bitterly, "is to leave Boston altogether." His brown eyes were glazed with exhaustion, and discouraged lines pulled down the corners of his mouth. Obviously, he hadn't slept, either.

Edgar Thornley pounded his fist on the table. The silverware clinked and jumped, and cream sloshed from the pitcher. "Leave Boston! How absurd!" he cried, slamming his fist again.

"Edgar!" Mrs. Thornley scolded. "There's no need for such behavior at the table."

"Yes, there is," he argued. "It's the only way I can get through my son's hard head!"

David glared at his father. "You've been running my life since I was born. Sending

these past months, except a bunch of letters?"

"It's my dream! Didn't you ever have a a dream, Papa?" David's normally mild brown eyes blazed.

"Yes, I did. To make a good home for my family. And to make certain that no son of mine would ever make a fool of himself!"

"Let me make my own mistakes. If I go into your bank, I'll become just like —" David broke off.

"Just like me, you were going to say? Is that so bad, son? Is it such a disgrace to be a respected member of the community? You want to throw that away and be a scruffy writer like that British fellow . . . what's-his-name."

"Charles Dickens," David supplied, the fight gone from his voice. "And I'd be proud to write half as well as he does."

Mr. Thornley grunted.

At that moment, Brooks came into the room, a bundle of mail under his arm. As the butler laid the mail at Mr. Thornley's place, Kathleen saw a large brown-paper package on top. David saw it, too; his face fell in dismay. They both knew what it was.

His father plucked the parcel off the pile and thrust it at David. "This is addressed to you, I believe. Open it."

With shaking fingers, David untied the twine and folded back the brown wrapping paper, revealing a sheaf of neatly written pages.

another person's mail was wrong, but she sensed David wouldn't mind, just this once.

A bank draft fluttered to the rug. The enclosed letter was indeed from the editor, who very much enjoyed David's story, "The Girl in the Fog," and was not only purchasing that story to publish in a forthcoming issue of the paper, but asked to see more of his work.

David had had a story accepted! And the publisher wanted more! He was on his way ... and he had done it with her special story!

Kathleen was bursting to tell David the news, but he had run off. No telling where he'd gone, he was so upset.

She decided to take the letter and bank draft upstairs to his room.

David's bedroom was decorated with white pine furniture painted a masculine burgundy-raisin color. The white muslin coverlet matched airy curtains stirring at the windows. There was a refreshing absence of clutter. The few personal belongings on the dresser top were arranged precisely, giving the impression that the occupant lived quietly, almost austerely. A real contrast to the opulence evident in the rest of the house.

Kathleen went over to the enormous walnut desk that stood under the double windows. Even here all was in order — the ink bottle resting beside a row of pen nibs and a jar of crow quills. A neat stack of papers — probably David's latest story — was pinned under a heavy crystal globe.

the room and attempted to snatch her pin from Victoria.

But the other girl coyly hid it behind her back. "*You* made this brooch? Next you'll be telling me you can fly."

"Give me my pin!"

Victoria shook her head sadly, as if she were about to do something she regretted. "I can't do that, Kathleen. I have to show this to my mother. She'll decide how to deal with a thief."

room. For that matter, you have no business in David's life, but it appears you've managed to get pretty close to him. Just last night, you lured him away from my party —"

"I did not! He found me. I never wanted to see him, that's why I hid."

"Well, you didn't hide very well. David would have spent the entire evening with you if Papa hadn't sent me to look for him. David didn't tell me you were behind those bushes, but I looked back once and saw you running toward the house."

Kathleen's palms felt icy. No matter how long she and Victoria argued in the doorway, the outcome would still remain the same. Victoria's accusation would ultimately lead to Kathleen's dismissal. She had no defense, no way of winning.

"My brother was clearly upset," Victoria went on. "You must have said something to him. After Papa announced David was joining him in the bank, David sulked the rest of the night."

"Maybe your father's announcement upset David. Not me."

Victoria flapped a careless hand. "Why should that bother him?"

Despite her anxiety, Kathleen was irritated by Victoria's attitude — pretending sisterly concern over David when she didn't even realize how much he wanted to be a writer. Kathleen knew she was going to be fired, so she said what she felt.

"Nobody in this house cares about anyone

Tessie bounded up the stairs two at a time, her face pink with excitement. "Kathleen! What's wrong with Miss Victoria? She flew past me a second ago, hollering for her mother. The missus came out of her sitting room like her petticoat was on fire. Victoria said she had to talk to her about you. What's going *on*, Kathleen?"

"Victoria was in our room this morning," Kathleen replied dully. "She found something of mine and now she's taking it to her mother."

"But why? What does she have?"

"The pin I wore on my dress last night."

"That moon-shaped thing? It's real pretty. You never said, but I figured your mother gave it to you."

Kathleen shook her head. "No, I made it myself." At Tessie's wide-eyed look, she added, "I haven't time to explain now. What's important is that Victoria thinks I stole the pin. That's what she's running to tell her mother."

"Stole it! Why, that's ridiculous! Everybody knows you wouldn't —" Tessie stopped as a red flush crept up her neck. "I should talk," she said sheepishly. "I almost did the same thing, just to get you in trouble. And now it's really happening. Kathleen, I feel so terrible."

"It's not your fault."

"Listen, if it'll help, I'll tell the missus you came here with that pin."

Kathleen sighed. "Thanks, Tessie. But I

sure. But you weren't by yourself. There are friends all around, Katie."

"Where? I didn't see anybody."

"You can't see them, but they can see you. They wouldn't let you get hurt, Katie. Or go hungry. Or get cold. They'd help you." He kissed the top of her upturned nose. "Remember, Kathleen O'Connor, you're never truly alone in this world."

Her hand on the knob, Kathleen smiled faintly at the recollection. How typical of Liam to cheer up a little girl with a story. Invisible friends! And yet part of her realized it wasn't entirely a fanciful notion. As long as she had memories of her family, of long evenings in Ireland, of Rory's sweet friendship, she really wasn't alone. And no one could take that away from her.

Her courage momentarily buoyed, Kathleen opened the door and went into the morning room to whatever awaited her.

Mrs. Thornley sat on the blue divan, tapping her short, pudgy fingers impatiently on the side table. Victoria stood with a triumphant gleam in her dark eyes.

"You wanted to see me, ma'am?" Kathleen asked politely.

"You can drop the innocent act," Victoria said.

Her mother waved in Victoria's direction. "Be quiet, please. Let me handle this. Kathleen, come here." When Kathleen crossed the room to stand before her, Mrs. Thornley de-

one of the footmen he hired for Victoria's party used to work down on the waterfront. This man saw you, Kathleen, and told Brooks he could have sworn you were the famous red-haired pickpocket who worked on the docks earlier this year. I was too busy then to think much of it."

"Pickpocket! Were you really?" Victoria stared at Kathleen with an expression of amazement bordering on admiration. Then she added. "It doesn't surprise me in the least. I wouldn't put anything past her, Mother."

"Victoria, I asked you to be still. I'm not finished with you, Kathleen. I have also been informed that you are interested in my son David. There are reports that you have been seen in his company, in various places. Now, are these stories true?"

An enormous lump blocked Kathleen's throat. How could she possibly answer that? *Yes, Mrs. Thornley, I'm guilty. I did all those things.* No matter what she said, she'd still be fired. And she doubted her employer would give her a letter of reference. Getting another job would be next to impossible.

So why should she confess anything? In fact, she didn't have to say a word if she didn't want to.

Holding out her hand, Kathleen said with more conviction than she felt, "If you'll give me my pin, Mrs. Thornley, I'll pack my clothes and leave."

Outraged, Mrs. Thornley got to her feet.

ever want to eat, plenty of servants to boss around so you never dirty your lily-white hands." Kathleen was aware that she was losing her own temper, which made her nearly as bad as Mrs. Thornley, but she didn't care. Feelings she had pent up for months exploded, and she couldn't stop now.

"You" — she pointed at Mrs. Thornley — "are the silliest, most useless woman I've ever known. When I think of how hard my mother worked and yet she was still kind and beautiful . . . well, you don't deserve to be mentioned in the same breath with her. If you walked out of this house today, no one would miss you, and by tomorrow your existence would be forgotten entirely —"

Victoria rushed to her mother's defense. "Don't you talk to her —"

But Kathleen whirled on her, turning the full effect of her fiery eyes on Victoria. "And you . . . you're worse than useless. At least your mother tends to a few household duties, but you don't do a thing, except dress up and spend money. A girl of your age and background, as your mother loves to toss in my face, should be going out every night of the week with eligible young men. But the truth is, only that puny Harold Huntley takes you out and only then because his parents make him!"

"That's enough!" Victoria cried.

But Kathleen went on. "You think because you're rich Americans you don't have to be nice to anyone but other rich Americans.

had she dusted that table, lovingly polished the tiny silver box? Now she'd never see those things again . . . or David. At least when she cleaned downstairs, she felt close to David, knowing he was in his room upstairs, writing at his desk.

And now it was all over.

There was nothing left to say. Kathleen turned and went up to the maid's room on the third floor. She pulled the box out from under her cot. Her worn wooden clogs lay in one half, along with the English grammar book. The old burlap sack was neatly folded in the other side. All she had brought from Ireland.

Shaking open the sack, she dropped in the shoes and book. Her ragged, brown wool dress hung limply from the peg rack. Kathleen put that into the bag also but left the green taffeta. The gown had never really been hers, anymore than she had belonged to this life.

The blue serge dress that Cook had cut down for her would serve her well, and she did have brand-new boots. Except for painful memories, she'd leave this house with more than she had come with.

Kathleen bent down to flip over the straw mattress. Tied to one of the ropes that supported the mattress was a cloth sack. Her wages. She unknotted the string, hefting the purse. It seemed a vast sum, more than her parents had ever owned at one time.

Another bundle hung from the bed frame, tied by a scrap of ribbon. A stiff spray of

cot and drew Pippa close to her. "My leaving has nothing to do with whether you are good or bad. You must stop trying to please everyone, do you understand? You are a good girl, better than you'll ever know, but you worry too much." She pushed back a strand of Pippa's hair and added in a softer tone, "Keep your doll, Pippa. And Oliver would be heartbroken without you. . . ."

"But you're my best friend," Pippa cried. "Who will I talk to now? Who will tell me stories?"

"Patrick will still be here. He can tell you all about fairies and leprechauns. More than I ever could." She hugged the thin body. "And David will talk to you. He'll — he'll take you places and give you pony rides. . . ."

They were both crying now.

"David will miss you most of all," Pippa whispered.

"Will he? I wonder."

"You might have been my sister."

Kathleen wiped a tear from the child's cheek. "Those are very sad words, aren't they? 'Might have been.'" Before emotion swept away her last shreds of reason, Kathleen kissed Pippa's forehead, picked up the sack, and fled the room.

If only she had time to say goodbye to Cook and Tessie. And Patrick. But the longer she delayed her leave-taking, the more she increased her chances of running into David. And he was the last person on earth she wanted to see.

Chapter
Twenty-two

THE wrought-iron gate loomed before her, all, imposing, the elegant scrollworked *T* in the center never letting her forget the family who lived within the spear-topped fence. Kathleen touched the latch. The gate swung inward on oiled hinges, opening as easily as she'd always imagined. She stepped through the gate, closing it quietly behind her.

Across Beacon Street, the Common spread its green lawns. Sunlight bronzed the stately elms and willows. Above the trees, a translucent, late-setting half moon — the same moon that poured pearly light over the party the previous night — hung on in the sky, as if reluctant to leave. A ring of children sat around the Wishing Stone. Kathleen envied them their ability to enjoy the hot July morning, untroubled and carefree.

By a trick of the light — or maybe an

The decision gave her new direction. She headed toward the docks without hesitation.

As she passed trim row houses, their soft peach-brick facades drawing warmth from the sun, Kathleen remembered the day Patrick led her through these same cobble-stoned streets, showing her a Boston far different from the dingy waterfront. She paused before a town house on the corner, charmed by lacy curtains framing the bow window, pots of petunias flanking the door-way, and the stone love seat in the tiny garden.

What a perfect house for two people in love, she thought wistfully. Without even seeing the occupants, she knew they were very happy. The whole house reflected it.

She walked on for quite some time, notic-ing that the streets sloped downward. Her pace picked up, as if her feet were now hurry-ing her to meet her destiny. She recognized the warehouses and taverns that comprised her world her first two weeks in Boston.

Mrs. McCracken's boardinghouse is right down there, Kathleen observed. She won-dered if little Jimmy Groats was still living there, earning his keep by stealing. She won-dered if Mrs. McCracken — "just like a mother," Dick Whistle once said — still served rice every day, supplemented with a little bacon on Sundays.

How grim life was in those days. She shud-dered at the horrible thought that she might still be there, too, picking pockets, evading

Kathleen could smell the sea before she actually saw it. The street lurched downhill, rushing dramatically toward the harbor. A forest of masts, circled by gulls, stuck up against the sky. Laplets of blue-gray water sparkled in the sun, like glimmers of secrets.

Before she approached the docks, Kathleen had to figure out her next move. She knew she didn't have enough money to buy her passage. She'd planned to pawn her pin at one of the dozen or so pawnshops lining the wharves, but since Victoria had taken her brooch, that was no longer possible. She could try to sell her good shoes and dress but suspected the price of her clothes wouldn't bring her that much closer to her goal.

No sense in even asking the passage brokers, she decided. Without full fare, she was no better off than the poor people who camped in doorways.

"Why is it that some people have more money than they can spend while others don't have enough to get by on?" she said aloud, indignant that conditions seemed worse than ever on the waterfront.

"Just the way things are," a man replied, smiling at her impudently.

Kathleen jumped. She'd forgotten that she had crossed an invisible line — down here on the docks the rules of society carried no weight. A strange man could speak to a girl and think nothing of his rudeness. Kathleen had grown used to the genteel, protective atmosphere at the Thornley mansion. Sud-

Kathleen pressed her lips together. Oh, no, you don't. Reverting to the pickpocket techniques she once learned, Kathleen tripped the runner as he flew by. Quick as a cat, she recovered the girl's bundle and handed it back to her, ignoring the man's jeers.

In Gaelic she told the girl, "Watch out for men like that one. Also people who claim they are from your county. They only want to steal what you have. If you're looking for a place to stay, go down to the end of that street and turn left. There's a big white house on the corner — a respectable boardinghouse just for women."

The girl said nothing but smiled her gratitude.

Kathleen stood there, watching the girl follow her directions with no further difficulty until she was out of sight.

This is all it takes, she thought. *Just a kind word in their own language. Some warning about what to expect. At least enough to get them started on the right foot. It can be done — but not by me.*

She had to find a boat bound for the British Isles. Worse, since she didn't have enough money for passage, she would have to stow away. The prospect of sneaking aboard a filthy cargo ship and hiding in the hold for several weeks filled her with dread. Yet there was no other way.

First, she had to buy a "sea-store" of provisions, enough to last her at least a month. Then she had to find the right ship.

Kathleen whirled around and melted into the crowd, hoping she was not drawing attention to herself. Behind her, several others took up the man's cries. It was only a matter of minutes, she knew, before a policeman would wade through the throng, calling for order.

She ran until a pain in her side forced her to slow down. Her heart thundered against her rib cage. For some reason she was as frightened as though she had picked the man's pocket herself. Did seeing Dick make her feel that guilty about her past, an unpleasant reminder of days she wished she'd never lived?

A gull screeched overhead, its shrill cry echoed by other birds wheeling around the tall mast of a ship on wings sharply lined against the sapphire sky.

Kathleen threw her head back to follow the birds. The gulls' aimless circling underscored her own lack of purpose. She started to cry. What was wrong with her? Did she want to go back to Ireland or not?

The inner voice that replied was small but firm.

No.

More than anything else in the world, Kathleen hated to take a step backward, to admit defeat. Running home to Ireland wouldn't solve anything, she realized. Once there, she'd be presented with a new set of problems. The old ones she refused to face would still be with her.

opened her eyes again. Church spires, the cupola of Faneuil Hall. The Cradle of Liberty. Suddenly, Kathleen wanted more than a taste of freedom. She wanted to make jewelry in Jack Thornley's shop. And she wanted to see David — just one last time to tell him how much she loved him.

"Hey!" an achingly familiar voice shouted above the dock traffic. Kathleen's heart leaped in recognition.

David! Her prayers had been answered!

The next few seconds passed in a blur. Kathleen's attacker tightened his grip as David raced up the gangplank, his hands balled into fists. With one well-aimed blow, David knocked the man's arm away from Kathleen. She fell against the rail, gingerly touching her bruised throat. Two more punches had the man doubled over, then David booted him over the side where he landed with a loud splash.

"If I were you, I'd start swimming," David threatened when the man surfaced, spewing a long stream of brownish water. "You so much as set foot in this town again and you'll be in jail before you've gone three steps!"

He turned to Kathleen, panting, his hair falling over his forehead. "Are you all right, Kathleen? Did he hurt you?"

She shook her head, then tested her voice. "I'm all right. My throat is sore, that's all. David, he was going to kidnap me!" she exclaimed, as shock gave way to realization. She began to shake uncontrollably.

what my father says." He paused, gazing into her eyes with such intensity that Kathleen held her breath, waiting for his next words.

"And the other decision I reached concerned you, Kathleen. You are the only girl for me . . . I've known from the first day I saw you holding Pippa's cat in the kitchen. You looked so beautiful in the firelight . . . your eyes as green as the cat's. I fell in love with you that very instant. But like a fool, I've made us both miserable because I was afraid to trust my own feelings. No wonder my early stories were so awful. They lacked substance, just as my life lacked meaning. When I met you, you showed me what was missing. I learned to search myself and draw out feelings I've suppressed since my parents sent me to school in Virginia. That's when I wrote the story about the girl in the fog. And now it's going to be published! I owe it all to you."

Kathleen shook her head. "Your talent is your own. I didn't do anything."

"But you have," David insisted. "You've turned my life around. That's why I panicked when Tessie told me you were fired. I came back to the house, ready to tell my father I had made up my mind about being a writer. Then I found your note and ran out so we could share the news. That's when Tessie told me you were gone." He stopped, and when he continued, his voice throbbed with emotion. "You can't imagine how terrible I

sive gold band would not slide off her knuckle. She had never seen a more wonderful sight than his ring on her finger.

"Will you?"

"I —" She felt dizzy. Things were moving too fast for her to comprehend. Only a little while ago, she was about to board a ship for Ireland. Like David, she had wandered until the truth had come to her: she really wanted to stay in America. And though she loved him, she never dreamed he'd look for her, much less ask her to marry him!

"I'll replace this with something that fits better," he said, apparently thinking her hesitation was caused by the ring. "I have a trust fund that I'll inherit in a few months, so we'll have enough money to live well. And there's a little row house in Beacon Hill that overlooks the river. It'll be perfect for us — unless you'd rather live somewhere else —"

"David, slow down! Let me catch my breath!" She nearly laughed at his enthusiasm. "You never told me what your mother said. And your *father!* He'll explode when he finds out!"

David grinned. "Sure he will. He always explodes when I do something other than what he wants. But he'll get over it. And so will my mother. Give them time, Kathleen. They'll come around. Once they get to know you, they'll love you. Just like I do."

"Well . . ." It would be difficult for a while. But she was a fighter; nothing David's parents ever said to her could possibly be as bad

emerald, lay Ireland. It was her home once, and she knew she'd never forget those days. But David was offering her a new life, an opportunity to grow and find her own talents.

Memories of Ireland would remain forever green, but America was now her home. She and David would live in one of those beautiful little houses. Kathleen would make lace curtains for the bow window and plant violets in the window boxes. When Pippa came to visit, Kathleen would tell her stories in the garden. And as often as possible, Kathleen would visit the immigrant ships, giving directions and extending hope.

She did not hesitate. As she had once told Tessie, life is too short.

"Yes," she said simply. "I will marry you."

The last thing Kathleen saw before David bent to kiss her was the gull sailing overhead. The sun caught the tilted wings and turned them to gold. Just like magic.

An exciting excerpt from the first chapter of MARILEE follows.

Marilee laughed softly. "I hear no complaints," she reminded him.

Indeed, who among the passengers or crew aboard the *Pryde* would complain about any wind that buffeted them along the Virginia coast? Having survived four perilous months at sea, the very sight of land brought a surge of joy and relief.

Certainly, Marilee had no complaint herself. On the contrary, when the first cry of "Land, Ho" had been shouted by the excited lookout in the crow's nest, she had flown up from the cabin she shared with her aging maid to be the first watcher at the rail.

She had not left that railing since, except when absolutely forced to. With Philip at her side most of the time, she had watched that slender, etched line on the horizon deepen and gain color and shape until now the land lay close.

Until the day she came aboard the *Pryde* for this passage, Marilee had spent the whole of her sixteen years on English soil. Now, as she stared at the green banks of the James, she had trouble remembering how it felt to step on firm land instead of balancing her slender weight against the swaying of the ship.

The wind gusted, loosening her hood to release more flying ringlets to whip around her face. She pursed her mouth and blew at them mightily, only to have them tumble back, obscuring her view. With a sigh she shoved them back under the hood of her

Yet since her father's death, she seemed to have lost her hold on joy. The smallest thing would fill her hazel eyes with tears, even as they were now.

And she must not let Philip see that sad face again. Before meeting this young officer of the *Pryde*, she had only known of him as her brother Matthew's dearest friend and agent. She had been astonished to find him so young, a man in his mid-twenties, lean and graceful, with sandy hair and deeply set eyes with a darkness that seemed bottomless in both their color and their expressiveness.

During this long sail he had become Marilee's own friend. She knew now how sensitive he was to a turn of phrase or a note of sadness in her voice. More than once on the voyage he had eased her grief with a perceptive word said in that deep and gentle voice of his.

And certainly Philip Soames must never know how much she dreaded this new life she was facing in the wilderness of Virginia. After all, her brother was opening his home to her; Philip himself had undertaken her welfare during this passage. How could she be so rude and ungrateful?

Yet the grief that had come at her father's death had been joined by a growing fear, a formless, dark mass of pain that pressed against her heart, leaving her sleepless through the long nights of the trip.

Conscious of her companion's sympathetic silence, she forced herself to smile for him.

will never see a gull floating on drafts of air without being reminded of you."

"The teacher learned more than the student," he told her. "Every growing thing will remind me of you, making me wonder if its leaves or bark hide the mystery of your healing art.

"Possibly," he went on, "it is just as well that you didn't bring some merry younger woman with you. You would have lost her the minute you landed at Jamestown. Some lonely Virginia planter would coax her to the altar as fast as the bans could be read. At least no one will steal Hannah from you."

Catching another wisp of that stubbornly flying hair, Marilee looked up at him. "All this talk of the scarcity of women in Virginia amazes me. After all, my brother found his wife here."

"Your brother Matthew Fordham is one of a kind," he told her. "Even as you are, Marilee."

Then, as if embarrassed by his own words, he returned to the subject of Hannah. "Well, so it is. Poor old Hannah. Now she must even change the name of her ailment. One cannot be seasick with the ocean behind us and the water of the James River ruffling past our prow."

"The James River," Marilee echoed softly. She leaned eagerly against the rail to stare across the frothy water toward the land.

How wide the James River was. How

talk. How long would it take her to get used to this constant talk of danger, of villages surrounded by stockades with guards and cannons against the world outside? She knew this must be necessary from having heard about the battles with the Indians, but being reminded of these dangers chilled her more than the cold wind ever could.

The din came from all directions, from above where the sailors shouted in the rigging and from around them on the deck, which teemed with activity. As the sails were trimmed for the dropping of the anchor, a swarm of small boats left the shore to swirl around the *Pryde.* Along the shore and the length of dock, crowds of people, some of them soldiers in scarlet pantaloons, jostled and waved, shouting hearty greetings that the sailors returned.

Philip said, "I believe your belongings are all packed and ready to take ashore."

Marilee nodded. Everything was ready but herself. How she envied Philip, who would spend only a few weeks in Virginia before getting to sail back to England. But then, Philip was different from herself. Philip had something to go back to; his work, his little flat that overlooked the river, and friends.

Marilee stole a glance at the tall young officer at her side. How well she knew him. How close they had drawn together in friendship.

At first she had felt that she had little to offer this man in return. What could she, a

From the first she had wondered why a man so attractive in every way had neither a wife nor a family. Then had come that magical night when, with the ship sleeping, he had whispered through the lock until she left her bed to come on board.

The moon had been a full, glowing orb that laid a path of light to the end of the world. Through it a school of giant whales was moving, churning the water to frothy lace, lifting fountains of light into the air with their great, gasping exhalations.

When those giants had passed, leaving the sea still again, he had talked to her about the loneliness of his life.

"I have thought of marriage," he had told her, carefully avoiding her eyes. "Each time my ship nears harbor, I see the joy and anticipation of other men and wonder how it would be to have some loving wife waiting for me, too." Then he shook his head. "But even if the woman lived who could fulfill my unreasonable dreams, I doubt if I would have had the courage to ask her to marry me. The wife of a seafaring man has no life to envy. All those months of prayer and fear and waiting." He fell silent for a moment before adding, "I remember too well my mother's grief, and my own."

Then he had turned to joking because, like herself, he was not a person who liked to spend words on unhappy, solemn talk. "Can a man who is not at home enough to keep a cat expect to satisfy a wife?"

so lovely as you could be joining his household."

"Beauty, indeed," she said. "Perhaps he will have a clearer eye than his friend Philip." Her tone was teasing, but her heart had fallen at his words. Matthew's household. "I don't know Abigail, his wife, either," she reminded Philip. "He married her here, you know, and I've never seen even so much as a drawing of her."

Marilee was conscious of his glance at her face and felt the comforting pressure of his hand on her arm. "You really are concerned about this, aren't you?" he asked.

Before she could reply, he went on heartily. "I'll help you. You are to study the faces in the crowd. The most handsome man you see there will be your brother."

Searching for Matthew's face, her attention was caught by a young man who was working his way through the crowd toward the dock. "The most handsome man you see," Philip had said. Surely there was no man under the sky of Virginia more handsome than this gentleman who smiled as he passed among the people on shore. She was not even sure that she had seen anyone more appealing in all of England.

Even from this distance she could catch the brightness of his smile as he spoke to people he passed. His mouth was wide and warm with humor under eyes that seemed to hold glints of laughter. Never, except on a

SUNFIRE™ ROMANCES

Spirited historical romances about the lives and times of young women who boldly faced their world and dared to be different.

From the people who brought you WILDFIRE®...

An exciting look at a NEW romance line!

Imagine a turbulent time long ago when America was young and bursting with energy and passion...

When daring young women defied traditions to live their own lives...

When heart-stirring romance and thrilling adventure went hand in hand...

When the world was lit by *SUNFIRE*...